RESTLESS

AN ANTHOLOGY OF
MUMMY HORROR

EDITED BY JIM BEARD & JOHN C. BRUENING

A Flinch Books Production

RESTLESS: AN ANTHOLOGY OF MUMMY HORROR
Copyright © 2017 by Jim Beard and John C. Bruening

SPECIAL EXHIBITS

UNWRAPPED TO KILL

Introduction

Let's all admit something: mummies have never really gotten their due.

Oh, sure, they've been around a for a few thousand years or so, and even starred in a few feature films here and there, but compared to vampires and werewolves and zombies, well, mummies kind of come up short in the popularity contest.

Restless is here to change that.

The fascination with mummies has long stemmed from a mixture of fact and fiction, with fact settling them in their resting places, and fiction forcing them up again for further duty. And to me, that's a lot of what makes these wrapped-up wonders so interesting: they're real. Now, that's not to say that vampires and werewolves and zombies don't have some roots in the real world, but in comparison mummies are completely grounded, so to speak. We didn't have to create them. They've existed right alongside us all this time.

And that's what makes them so horrifying.

To my mind, the best horror fiction concerns reality; commonplace things that are supposed to be inanimate getting up and walking among us. That's how mummies can become more than just the hobgoblins of our imagination.

My own fascination with them was cemented courtesy of a mummy that was on view in my hometown art museum, among its ancient Egyptian art and antiquities display. It rested in a glass case, a small thing—probably a child or a very short adult—but it drew my very young self to it every time I walked into that room. I would stare at it for long minutes, pressing my hand against the glass, wondering what the wrappings would feel like...and wondering what it might be thinking as it lay there, silent and stony.

1

Wait. Did it just move? Was that a bit of dust that fell from it, because it shifted its head just a smidge?

See what I mean? Horrifying.

That particular mummy is gone now, taken off view in a twenty-first century nod to sensitivity, but its ghost lingers on in me, fueled by decades of Universal Monsters films and yes, a few pages of prose fiction. But not enough. Not enough to suit us here at Flinch. So we did something about it.

Restless was conceived as an opening salvo in a new era of mummy horror fiction, designed not only to tell new tales of shambling crypt-kickers from ancient Egypt, but also from other points across the globe. Mummies are not limited to the shores of the Nile, of course, and this book intends to open up tombs and graves and caves to find desiccated corpses of other cultures, too.

Why should the old pharaohs have all the fun?

So, get all wrapped up in your favorite reading chair and crack the seal on the six stories that follow these meager words of introduction. We've arranged your own personal unwrapping party with a half-dozen of the best storytellers in the modern pulp fiction universe, each one of them illuminating a few dark corners of their twisted minds to bring you mummies in a new light.

Jim Beard
Co-Founder, Flinch Books

LOVE'S DEADLY KISS

by Barry Reese

T homas York brushed the dirt off his shirt as he waited on the
doorstep of Sellas Manor. He was newly arrived from the Dark
Continent, where he had spent the better part of the past two years.
To say that the experience had changed him forever was an under-
statement. He had returned to England with a renewed appreciation
for modern conveniences, though he suspected he would never feel
completely clean again. That sense of being unwashed went beyond
his battered clothing, sinking all the way down to his soul.

The door opened for the second time in the past five minutes.
The face of Dinkins, the aged butler, was now replaced by a far more
attractive one, belonging to a young blonde woman no older than
twenty-five. Her fine figure was outlined in a lovely dress that probably cost more than all of York's belongings put together.

"Yes?" she asked, narrowing her eyes. "Dinkins says you're here
to see my husband?"

York could scarcely hide his surprise. "You're married to Charles?"

"I am. And you are…?"

"Thomas York." He gave what he hoped was a stately bow but
he was quite conscious that a puff of dust and dirt went flying when
he bent over. When he straightened, he gave her a generous smile.

"I have consulted with your husband in the past. I tried to be back in time for his recent birthday celebration but circumstances didn't allow that. He sent me an invitation."

York fumbled about in the pocket of his coat. He drew forth a dirty envelope and saw her eyes flick disapprovingly over it. "I'm sorry," he said. "But I don't believe I caught your name...?"

"I didn't give it, Mr. York." She took a step back, having apparently decided that she had no choice but to give him permission to enter. "My husband will no doubt be overjoyed to see you. He's locked away in his study. I'll show you the way."

"Oh, there's no need. I've been here often enough, though it's been a few years." York entered the foyer, noting that the interior had changed somewhat. Gone were the large framed maps and wildlife images that he remembered—in their places were paintings of flowers and well-dressed ladies at rest. "I see the house has the unmistakable fingerprints of a woman upon it," he said with a chuckle. When she didn't share in the humor, he added, "The changes are most welcome."

She sighed rather dramatically before saying, "My name is Charlotte, Mr. York. Now please go in to see my husband. He mentioned your name once or twice to me and I believe he was very saddened that you missed his birthday."

Charlotte turned and walked away without another word, leaving York to marvel at her. She was far, far younger than Charles. In fact, she could have been his granddaughter! Still, the old man deserved happiness in whatever form he chose it. He had never married nor had children as a younger fellow, and so he'd been alone in this marvelous house for far too long. York would begrudge him nothing.

As York made his way to the study, he noted other changes that had been made to the décor. Gone were the dusty old rugs and marble statues of breast-baring maidens. The decidedly feminine touch that had appeared in their place was a bit off-putting to York, who was a bachelor of long standing.

He found the study quickly enough and noted that the door was closed. He paused before knocking, thinking he heard Charles engaged in conversation with someone. But after a moment, he heard no response and assumed that Charles must have been muttering to himself. He gave a quick rap with his knuckles and a brief second later, the door was opened, revealing his old friend. They hugged and exchanged pleasantries before York entered the room, and Charles shut the door behind him. This room, at least, seemed untouched by the young Mrs. Sellas. It was just as much a jumble of papers and knickknacks as it had been during York's last visit.

Charles offered brandy and York accepted. There was a rose to the old man's cheeks that was unmistakable. "You're in love, aren't you?" York asked.

Charles paused and looked somewhat embarrassed, like a schoolboy whose crush had been revealed. "It's that obvious, is it?"

"Yes…and that's a good thing. She's quite beautiful."

"You've seen her?" Charles asked in confusion. He handed York a glass filled to the brim.

"Of course. She met me at the door and told me where to find you."

Charles shook his head and took a large drink from his own glass. "Oh, you mean Charlotte. Yes, she's pretty enough." He cleared off papers from a couple chairs and offered one to York.

When they were seated, York leaned forward and whispered conspiratorially. "Charles, who else would I speaking of? Are you… are you seeing another woman?"

Charles smiled and paused before answering. "It's not what you're thinking, I assure you. I'll introduce you to the other woman in my life in a moment. But first, tell me about Africa. What was it like?"

"Hot." York sat back and shook his head. "You know I went there to investigate some of the stories about human sacrifice in the Congo. I found more than I bargained for—a whole cult that worshipped a dark goddess intent on devouring not just human flesh but the entire world."

"Details, man!"

"I'm still trying to sort it all out, Charles. I haven't even started putting my notes in order for the book yet. I promise you'll get a look at it even before my publisher does."

Charles beamed. "I've always been jealous of your life, my boy. Traveling the world, having adventures… all the while I'm trapped here in this house, attending social functions that bore me to death! I live vicariously through you."

"It can't be all that terrible. You're wealthy enough to never want for anything, your property is lovely and you've got a young wife who's put the color back in your cheeks. There are men who would die for all that you have."

"The house is too drafty in the winter and too hot in the summer. I can't get a damned thing to grow on the back half of the property. And money can't buy a man happiness."

York frowned. He remembered that Charles was prone to fits of depression, but this seemed to be a different sort of malaise. "Surely, Charlotte has brought some measure of happiness to you? Your vitality certainly seems much improved."

"Charlotte is beautiful, that is true. But I have no fantasies about the state of our marriage, Thomas. She is here for one reason and one reason only: my money! In return, she allows me to paw at her upon occasion but nearly so often as she allows our gardener to do the same."

York was appropriately shocked and made no effort to hide it. "She's cuckolding you in your own home? Why do you stand for it?"

"I'm not as young as I used to be. Even if I were of a mind to, I couldn't keep up with her young passions. Besides, I have other things with which to occupy myself, and if her dalliance keeps her out of my study, all the better." Charles stood up and gestured for York to follow. "Let me show you what puts a smile on my face these days—and I do have Charlotte to thank for it, so that's another reason I allow her to take her pleasures where she may."

York followed along, pausing only briefly. There was a small mirror on the mantle, surrounded by old books and moldy papers. He saw himself and Charles together for a moment. They couldn't have looked more different. Charles was an old man with a slightly stooped posture. His hair was mostly gone now, revealing a liver-spotted scalp. His clothes were immaculate, however, and there was something in his bearing that spoke of good breeding. Meanwhile, York looked somewhat shabby in expensive clothing that had seen far better days in the past. His blond hair was just a tad too long, covering his ears, and his face, which had often been described as handsome, looked gaunt after years spent in Africa.

"Here she is," Charles said, yanking open a set of folding doors. York turned away from the mirror and hurried over, not sure what he expected to see. The upright figure within the small closet was certainly breathtaking… it was a female form, arms folded over an ample chest. Her entire body was swathed in ancient bandages. The form rested within a sarcophagus, its lid opened to reveal its inhabitant.

"A mummy…?"

"Yes! Charlotte gave her to me for my birthday. She knows my peculiarities as well as anyone and thought I'd enjoy owning her. She expected me to throw one of those 'unwrapping' parties, but I'm not going to. I wouldn't shame her like that."

"Shame who? Charlotte?"

"No! Her."

York looked back at the mummy, his eyes moving slowly up and down. He had seen other mummies before, but always in museums. Those had looked shriveled and somewhat ill-formed. This one, though, looked like a woman in the full bloom of health, only hidden behind cloth. "Are you certain this is legitimate?" he asked. "Not to be too uncouth about it, but her shape…"

Charles laughed. "I know what you mean. You can't be a red-blooded male and not take notice of her…attributes!"

"Quite so."

"She's a real mummy, Thomas… dating back to the days of ancient Egypt. I've spent hours in here studying her, listening to the tales of what life was like back then. It's intoxicating, learning about those days. I think I was born in the wrong time."

York looked puzzled. "Listening?"

"Hmm?"

"You said you studied her and 'listened.' What do you mean?"

"Oh," Charles shook his head. "You have to forgive me. It was a poor choice of words." He looked back at the mummy and York felt a chill run down his spine. The way his friend looked at the corpse was…not quite right. "I just meant that I stare at her, and when I do, I can almost feel the Egyptian sun beating down upon me. I can hear the cries of the slaves as they haul the rocks into place to build the great pyramids. And I can almost imagine her sitting in the lap of luxury, surveying it all."

"You think she was someone important?"

"I have no doubt." Charles closed the folding doors, hiding the mummy from sight. "You're going to stay a few days, aren't you?"

"Well, I need to get back to London to put some affairs in order and begin work on my book. My editor is a bit impatient with me."

"I insist you stay overnight. It's been so long since you've visited, and I'm sure you'd like a home cooked meal." Charles wagged a finger at his friend. "No arguments."

York grinned. "You shall get none from me. Thank you."

"I'll have a room prepared for you… and I insist that you give me your clothes to have the staff wash them. Or burn them. Whichever they feel is appropriate. I have some items that used to belong to my nephew—they'll fit you just fine."

"You don't have to go those lengths, Charles."

"I do! You look dreadful, and Charlotte will expire from the shame of it all if you attend dinner looking like that." He eyed York's hair with obvious disapproval. "And I'll send Dinkins round with the shears, as well."

York sighed good-naturedly, knowing when it was best to let his friend have his victories. "As you see fit," he finally relented. He clasped Charles on the shoulder, noticing how thin and frail the man felt beneath his hand. Charles was aging fast, even with the fine color in his cheeks. "It's good to see you again."

~ ~ ~

After a bath and trim, York felt revitalized. He had changed into

10

a crisp white shirt, a blue vest and dark trousers. His own boots had been polished and returned to him, but otherwise every bit of clothing he wore was new to him. The fit wasn't exact but York didn't mind. The slight looseness of the shirt gave him freedom of movement that pleased him.

York was still worried about Charles, and when Dinkins had visited to trim his hair, he had broached the subject of the household's current state. He hadn't expected much in return as Dinkins had always been a taciturn fellow, but to his surprise, the old butler had seemed pleased to have the opportunity to unload his worries.

According to Dinkins, the stresses in the household had reached a breaking point prior to his employer's birthday. Charles had confronted his wife about the infidelities, which Dinkins seemed to imply consisted of more than just the gardener, and the subsequent row had nearly torn the marriage apart. After the presentation of the mummified "gift," things had settled down. Charles remained in his study all hours of the day and night, sometimes even taking his meals in there, while Charlotte was left with the freedom to follow her desires, be they shopping or carnal.

"Do you like her?" I had asked, surprised by his willingness to indulge in conversation.

His response had been unequivocal. "No, sir. I do not."

~ ~ ~

York was on his way to dinner when he heard whispered voices around the corner. He recognized one of the speakers as Charlotte, so he slowed his pace and stopped just before moving into view. He felt a bit silly eavesdropping, but given the tense relations in the house and his loyalty to Charles, he felt justified in his actions.

"He invited that horrid man to stay the night," Charlotte was saying, and York had no doubt that he was the "horrid man" to which she was referring.

A man's gruff voice replied, "You think he's going to be a problem?"

"I don't know. Apparently he's some sort of writer, but Charles seems to think he's also an adventurer. He's much slighter than you, though. I don't think he'd be a threat."

York frowned. What exactly were they planning? It certainly had sinister implications.

Their conversation ceased and he heard the unmistakable sounds of kissing. Then they separated, their footsteps going in different directions. When he was confident that he was not in danger of being detected, York moved on towards dinner but his mind was greatly occupied. During his time in Africa, much of his waking hours had been spent worrying over supernatural matters. He had feared for not only his life but for his very soul. Returning to England was meant to be a relaxing affair, an opportunity to remind himself of the beauty and rhythm of the "natural world."

Instead, he'd found his friend caught up in a web of deceit and potentially worse.

He passed by Charles' study and stopped. He could hear his friend moving about inside, whispering soft words that sounded almost sweet. It was a feminine voice, somewhat husky in tone. He couldn't quite make out what was being said. Had Charlotte come here after leaving her lover in the hall?

The door opened suddenly and Charles blinked in surprise. "Thomas?"

"I was about to knock and see if you wanted to walk with me to dinner," York replied smoothly. He'd learned to lie with ease in his life. It wasn't something he was particularly proud of, but it had certainly saved his skin on occasion. "Did I hear Charlotte in there with you?"

"No, it must have been your imagination, my boy." Charles patted his younger friend on the shoulder and set off down the hall. York stared back at the closed door to his study for a brief second before joining him. "You look much more like your old self," he added.

"Thank you. I feel much more civilized as well." York fell silent and Charles glanced at him with concern.

"I know that look," Charles said. "You have something weighing upon you."

"Your wife's affair with the gardener—I'm afraid I can't put it out of my mind. It's not right, Charles. You should confront her and demand that it end…or you'll divorce her."

"You're not married yet, Thomas, so the concept of it in your mind is still full of fiction. Real life isn't a fairy tale. Men and women get what they need out of a relationship and become partners in their union. I daresay more marriages have adultery as a part of their existence than don't."

"I would hope not!" York exclaimed. "Surely the majority of people take their vows more seriously than that."

"I admire your youthful idealism," Charles said with a chuckle. "I don't doubt that you'll find that kind of marriage, Thomas. You're a good man—and still a young one. It's not as easy for me at this stage in my life to find a charming companion."

"Perhaps you merely needed to look for someone closer to your own age?"

"I like young women, what can I say? I did when I was young and I still do now that I'm old and gray."

The friends reached the dining room and found that Charlotte was already seated. She had not waited for the men to join her before starting on her soup. There was something in that small, seemingly insignificant gesture that told York everything he needed to know about the state of their relationship. She didn't consider him worthy of even the most conventional of social graces.

Dinner consisted of excellent food and short, perfunctory conversation. Charles asked York a few details about life in Africa, but Charlotte was obviously eager to be free of their company. Strangely, York sensed that Charles felt the same. He mentioned in passing a need to return to his study for more "work," though York seemed confident that he merely wanted to spend more time with his ghoulish prize.

When the niceties were over and the party had finished dessert, Mr. and Mrs. Sellas said goodnight to each other and to York before vanishing in two different directions. York was literally left sitting by himself in the dining room.

He ended up wandering around the house, examining the new furnishings and wondering why he felt so ill at ease. Was it just shock over the state of his friend's marriage? The somewhat dire implications of Charlotte's conversation with her lover? Or was it merely that after years away from civilization and its carefully tended webs of deceit that he no longer felt home among its tenants? Perhaps, he mused, it would be better to vanish back into the wilds, the dark places of the world, and let the shadows envelop him.

His pondering came to an abrupt end as he was leaving one of the house's many sitting rooms, this one decorated with several fine China tea settings. He heard a heavy thump, followed by a muffled cry and the breaking of glass. Years of living on the edge of danger had honed his senses to a keen point and he burst into action, sprinting down the hallways in search of the sound. He knew instinctively from whence it had come: Charles' study.

When he got there, the found the door locked and one of the maids approaching with a fearful cast to her features. "Do you have a key?" he demanded.

When she answered in the negative and said she'd have to fetch the butler, York knew he had no time to waste. He kicked in the door on the first try and entered the room. He found Charles on the floor, the back of his head a bloody mess. A shattered vase lay beside him and the small closet that contained the mummy was open. The wrapped form seemed to stare balefully down at the macabre scene. York noticed that a window leading into the room was broken as well, and that the majority of the shattered glass fragments were inside on the carpeted floor. This told him that someone had burst in, as opposed to out. He made this assessment within seconds.

York knelt beside his friend and checked for a pulse. There was none. He was cursing under his breath when Dinkins arrived, slightly out of breath. The maid had roused him from his private chambers and for the first time, York saw him when he was not at his best. The butler's normally impeccable appearance was now marred by uncombed hair and a small trace of marmalade on his lower lip.

"My word!" the butler exclaimed. He came forward hesitantly

14

and asked, "Should I summon a doctor?"

"The authorities, I should say," York replied. He gently closed Charles' eyes and stood up. "The poor man's dead." He gestured meaningfully towards the shattered window. "Foul play, obviously."

"I should go and wake the missus."

York held up a hand to stop Dinkins from leaving. "Quickly, now—look around. You probably know these rooms better than I do. Is anything missing?"

Dinkins cast a slow glance about him, carefully avoiding looking at the dead body on the floor. York didn't begrudge him yet. Death was an awful thing, and the sad truth was that he'd seen so much of it that he was now able to look past its presence.

"No, sir. If something was taken, I'm not aware of it."

York nodded and let the help hurry away. He was fairly certain that Charlotte was already wide awake, though she would feign the opposite. The conversation he had overheard earlier now made perfect, chilling sense. Charlotte had been discussing the murder of her husband. He could tell that to the authorities, of course, but there were problems. One, he had no evidence other than his own word, and two, as an outsider, it would be very easy to have suspicion cast in his own direction. The fact that he was the first to discover the body would be used against him if he were painted as the villain of the piece.

A rustle of fabric and the soft exhalation of breath made the hairs on the nape of York's neck stand on end. He whirled about, wondering if Charlotte had entered without him knowing. Something in the sound had been feminine, though no one had spoken. York was still alone, save for the body of his friend…and the mummy.

He stepped towards the ancient corpse, noting how meticulously clean her wrappings were. Charles' work, no doubt, but it gave the impression that she was recently bound, and the full, supple curves of her body made him wonder how intact she was beneath the bandages.

York took several steps towards the mummy and a word blossomed in his mind, unfolding like an origami swan being disassembled. The word was "Ahset," and York immediately knew that it was not some random collection of letters… it was a name and it belonged to the woman before him.

York looked back towards the shattered door, making sure that no one was there to see his next actions. He approached the mummy and whispered, "Ahset?"

He paused, not sure what he expected to happen next. Would she somehow move, proving that Charles had not been insane? Was she actually alive under the wrappings, despite all common sense pointing in the other direction?

Footsteps in the hall distracted him and he frowned, feeling foolish. He started to turn away from Ahset when he heard that same rustling sound again, the one that had initially brought his attention round to the Egyptian woman's form. This time he was positive that he detected a change. Her right hand, crossed over her left breast, was at a lower angle than before. While it might be explained away as some trick of gravity, York felt certain that this was not the case.

Charlotte burst into the room, looking suitably distraught. She rushed to her husband's side, falling to her knees in dramatic fashion. She wailed and clutched at his still form in perfect imitation of despair.

York was not fooled in the least.

He looked back at Ahset, his eyes narrowed. What was happening here? He had seen the bizarre… the obscene… the hidden underbelly of the universe that normally did not move out into the light. Even so, the existence of a living mummy was enough to boggle the mind.

"Who would do such a thing?" Charlotte was asking.

York ignored her. The authorities would arrive soon enough, and there would be plenty of time to hear her sobbing at that time. Accusations would no doubt be leveled at York eventually, but in the meantime, he had no time to waste.

When he spotted Dinkins, he told the butler to keep everyone out of the study and to erect some sort of makeshift barrier across the shattered door to help. The body couldn't be moved until the police arrived, but York wanted to keep Ahset from prying eyes. He closed the doors over her little closet and hurried out into the hall, heading outside.

Charles' killer was still on the property, and York intended to find him.

~ ~ ~

The gardener's name was John, and he had been employed by Charles Sellas for nearly eight years. During that time he'd come to appreciate the old man. He had been firm but fair, and he never hesitated to dole out the praise for a job well done. Everything had changed when Charlotte had started coming around. John had found her lovely from the start and the long, lingering gazes she returned were full of passionate promises that were eventually fulfilled when they began a torrid affair. John felt guilty about cuckolding his employer, but Charlotte's body was impossible to deny.

It was she who first broached the subject of murder.

At first he'd balked, but she had a way of making him change his mind. And the promises about eventually splitting the family fortune were too much for him to resist. What man could truly say he'd turn down a beautiful woman and a fortune? Yes, it involved killing someone who had never done him wrong, but John persuaded himself that Charles probably only had a few years left on this earth regardless. All he was doing was pushing the process along a bit.

John scrubbed his hands in a bucket of water, staining it a light pink. He had intended to kill Charles without bloodshed, but the old man had put up more of a struggle than he'd expected.

John pulled off his torn shirt and tossed it into a waste bin, covering it with some other trash. He'd burn it all later. After putting on a clean shirt, he seized the handle of the bucket and stepped outside into the night, tossing the bloody water into a flowerbed.

He was returning to the modest quarters he called his home when York emerged on the path. John recognized the look of righteous fury in the man's eyes. John reacted instinctively, throwing the bucket at York's head. York knocked it aside, but John was already on the move, sprinting toward the main house. Under cooler circumstances, John would have realized that he'd have been better off denying culpability and disposing of the last bit of evidence—the ripped shirt—as soon as possible. Instead, he had confirmed his guilt by running.

York gained ground quickly. Years spent on the African savannah had honed his body and trained him in the best methods of attacking his prey. Though John knew the property far better than York did, this advantage was neutralized by the fact that John was in full panic mode.

York saw the main house coming into view, its lights plainly visible in the dark night. He wasn't sure what John's plan was, if there truly was one. Did he think that Charlotte would someone protect him? If so, he was bound to be wrong on that account. York had no doubt that Charlotte would cut her ties with him when they were no longer convenient.

York hurled himself in the air, landing hard upon the gardener's back. The two men hit the ground and York refused to give John a chance to strike back. Two hard blows to the back of John's head left the man unconscious.

Rising to his feet, York cursed the turn of events. He had hoped to catch John alone so that he could possibly convince the man to turn against Charlotte. He hadn't expected the gardener to bolt like this.

"Sir! Are you all right?"

York looked to his left to see Dinkins striding quickly towards him, concern etched on his face. "I'm fine," said York, "but I believe that John here has confessed his involvement in the murder."

"Oh, my," Dinkins whispered, covering his mouth and staring at John in disbelief. He recovered his dignity quickly and added, "The authorities should be here soon. Should we lock him up in the meantime?"

"A wise suggestion, my good man." York did most of the heavy work in lifting John off the ground, though Dinkins assisted by opening the doors to allow them inside. After tying John's hands, they dumped him into the study, not far from the body of the man he'd killed. Just before they exited the room, York noticed that the closet containing Ahset was opened slightly… he remembered closing it but perhaps Charlotte had looked inside?

Perhaps.

~ ~ ~

York found Charlotte in the dining room, taking tea. Her eyes were not red from crying as they should have been, confirming his suspicion that her behavior had merely been theatrics.

"The way you bolted from the scene, Mr. York, I was afraid that you were gone for good." The way she said this made York feel like his role as the scapegoat would have only been improved had he not returned.

"Actually, I went after your husband's killer." He leaned on the dining room table, fixing his steely gaze upon hers. "I found him, too."

Charlotte raised an eyebrow. "Really?"

"It's John, the gardener. And get this: he says that you and he were having an affair, and that you put him up to it." York kept his voice level, hoping she wouldn't see through his lie.

Impressively, Charlotte didn't take the bait. "That's so absurd. First of all, I would never betray my beloved husband in such a manner. Second, John is known for being a liar and a scoundrel. He would say anything to try to avoid being imprisoned. I'm afraid you've been played for a fool, Mr. York."

"I'm not sure the constable will see it that way" York replied. His voice betrayed his disappointment, and he was chagrined to see a small smile touch Charlotte's full lips before she composer herself.

The young Mrs. Sellas stood up. "This has been such a stressful event. I think I should retire to my room for a bit. Where did you imprison John?"

"He's somewhere safe and sound."

Charlotte nodded and strode from the room as though she were the Queen herself. York was left steaming in her wake, and he cursed himself for being a fool. She was crafty, that one. She was right, though. Even if John did admit to her role in the affair, it was the word of one groundskeeper against a wealthy, beautiful member of the upper crust. In England, that was hardly a fair fight.

A blood-curdling scream caused York to jump in alarm. It took a few seconds for him to orient himself, but when he realized where the cry had come from, the blood froze in his veins. Once again, he set off down the hall towards the study.

What he found defied rational explanation.

John was on the floor, still bound by the wrists and ankles. His head had been twisted completely around and his face was frozen in terror. The sarcophagus where Ahset had been housed was standing empty and there were small bits of cloth along the floor, leading towards the hall. The odds and ends of furniture that Dinkins had placed in front of the door to bar entry had been shoved aside, some of them laying on their sides.

As before, Dinkins and the servants arrived soon after York. They were kept out of the room by York, who didn't want a panic. "John is dead," York said simply. "Another murder."

Dinkins looked pale and shaky. "My heavens."

"How long before help arrives?"

"We sent a messenger, sir, and they've already returned. They said the constable would be along as soon as possible, but that they were involved in an affair in town and it might be a bit."

York muttered an African curse under his breath. "Check all the doors and then gather everyone in the house. Get all the servants into the dining room. Until this is sorted out, I don't want anyone to be alone. I'll go get Charlotte and we'll join you."

Without waiting for the old man to reply, York moved toward Charlotte's bedroom. His mind was awash with possibilities. Despite the strange things he had seen in Africa, he refused to accept that Ahset had someone survived the centuries. But if she hadn't murdered John, then who had? And how had they managed to move Ahset's body so quickly?

He paused outside her door, wondering how he should approach it. Deciding that honesty would be the best policy this time, he rapped strongly on the door and then waited.

Charlotte opened it a moment later, dressed in a silken nightgown that clung to her body. York could almost see how John could be so easily taken in by her.

"Mr. York, what a surprise. Has the constable arrived?"

"You obviously don't expect him tonight or you wouldn't be dressed for bed."

"I know him. He doesn't like to come this far out after dark. He'll come up with one excuse after the other to put it off. Then he'll show up shortly after breakfast. Besides, there's no hurry, is there? You've captured the murderer and nothing will bring poor Charles back to life." She lowered her voice at this last bit, trying to put off that she was broken-hearted.

"Stop the games," York snapped. "No one else is here, so you can be truthful. You married Charles for his money and you arranged to have him killed."

Charlotte suddenly shifted her body language and tone, becoming the ice queen that York already knew her to be. "Go away, Mr. York. There's nothing more for you to do here. I'm going to get away with it, and if you stay here until the morning, I might even be able to convince the authorities that it was you all along. Perhaps you went insane while out in Africa and returned to slay my poor husband? Sounds like a good yarn to me."

"Someone else is trying to write a new ending."

"What do you mean?"

"John's dead and Ahset is missing."

Charlotte looked genuinely shocked. "John is dead?" She took a step back before recovering herself. "Who is Ahset?" she asked, looking up at him with narrowed eyes.

"The mummy."

"She has a name?"

"Yes. Look, that's not important. What is important is that there's still a murderer in this house." He reached out to seize her by the elbow. "We're all gathering together in the dining room for protection."

"But one of them could be John's killer! I'm safer locked in my room!"

"Don't be daft, woman! Charles and John were both alone when they were murdered, weren't they? We stand a better chance of survival by watching each other."

Something in his manner finally breached Charlotte's defenses. She stared hard at him before allowing heralded to be led down the hall. "You're serious, aren't you? You think I'm in danger!"

"Yes, I do."

A chill wind blew through the corridor, rustling Charlotte's nightclothes and sending a shiver through her supple body.

York paused, stopping so suddenly that Charlotte bumped into him. "Do you smell that?" he asked.

Charlotte flared her nostrils, picking up on what he meant. In addition to the sudden cold that permeated the hallway, there was a strange odor—like an unusual mixture of female sweat and aged paper. The gender quality was immediately clear to both Charlotte and York. This was not the musky smell of a man but rather the scent of an unwashed woman. It was not entirely unpleasant, at least not to York, but it was certainly different from the heavily perfumed female at his side.

"What's happening?" Charlotte asked, her voice quavering.

York was about to reply that he didn't know, when he noticed another peculiarity—a thick fog rushing towards them from the turn of the hallway. It swelled up like a hand to envelop them, trapping them in a cool and somewhat moist embrace. The smell was much stronger now and York gasped, finding it hard to breathe.

"Your bedroom," he wheezed.

The two of them started to turn but a female voice brought them both to a halt. "Running will not save you."

York stared into the fog, seeing the silhouette of a woman. She was shorter than Charlotte, but her curves were more ample and her hair hung loosely about her shoulders. The scent was stronger now, growing with every step that she took toward them.

Charlotte screamed and pulled free of York's grip. She bolted towards her room and York heard her slam the door shut behind her.

"It's not possible," York whispered. His sanity threatened to shatter as Ahset came into view. Her body was mostly nude, though strips of burial cloth clung to her breasts, hips and legs. Her hair was raven-black and she wore elaborate makeup that accentuated her lovely eyes.

"And yet it is true," Ahset replied, a dangerous smile on her lips.

"How can you speak English?"

"Of all that you have seen, my ability to speak your tongue is what you choose to focus on?"

York refused to back off. "It's just one more thing that makes me believe this is some elaborate fraud."

"You heard me speak before, did you not?" Ahset closed her mouth but her words continued – directly into York's brain. *I am Ahset the Accursed. That is what they called me when the Pharaoh demanded that I suffer.*

York gasped.

Yes. I can read your mind. I was a priestess in life, gifted with the powers of the gods. The Pharaoh coveted my beauty, and when I refused him, he had my protégé betray me. I have existed for centuries in an awful state of half-life. I could hear all that occurred around me, but I could not communicate—not until Charles. He was different. He could sense that I was still alive. He cared for me and told me of his troubles. His attention fed me and gave me strength.

Ahset looked away, and for a moment she appeared so forlorn that York ached for her pain. She was the loveliest woman he had ever seen, and despite the unreality of her very existence, he felt like he could understand how Charles had become smitten with her.

"What is it… that you want?" he stammered at last.

Ahset replied with scorn, "Revenge. I want to see her suffer the way she made Charles suffer."

"And then?"

Ahset shrugged her bare shoulders. "Then I will go out into the world. There are so many things to see, so much to explore." She looked into his eyes and her lips curled into a smile. "Would you like to be my guide?"

York felt the tug of her sensuality, but there was something wrong, something about her that set him on edge. It wasn't the fact that she'd killed John. York had taken his share of human lives before, and he wasn't squeamish. The justice system was well and good, but there were times when the laws of man were not enough to punish the guilty. "There's something you're not telling me," he said. "You're painting yourself as the victim, but I'm not sure I believe that."

There was a pause and then Ahset laughed. The sound was deeply disturbing to York, and he took a step back in response. "You are wise. I was greatly feared in my time because of my power—and my cruelty. The Pharaoh both desired and hated me because of that. So he conspired to betray me." She ran her fingertips along her slender belly and between her breasts. "Serving me can be quite rewarding, however."

York shook his head, feeling as if invisible cobwebs were fogging his thoughts, just as surely as the mist was rising about his legs. "No…" he murmured.

His refusal sparked visible anger in Ahset and she lashed out with startling speed. The back of her closed fist struck him on the chin and drove him hard into the wall. He slumped to the floor, seeing stars. A bit of blood oozed from his clenched lips and his tongue ached.

Ahset stared down at him for a moment. York was only dimly aware of her presence, and by the time his mind cleared enough to focus on the danger of his situation, she was gone.

York pulled himself back to his feet and spat on the floor. He had bitten his lip when she struck him and he could already feel a bruise developing on his chin. She was immensely powerful, far more than a woman of her size should be.

Had Charles unwrapped her in private? Had he coupled with that…thing? Despite her beauty, she was not human. And despite the parts of her story that cast her as the innocent in this affair, York felt certain that she was a danger. Even if she had been kind in life, centuries of being unable to move or speak would drive anyone insane.

Charlotte's screams of terror reached York and spurred him out of his macabre reverie. He heard the splintering of wood as well, and York knew what the sound meant: Ahset was breaking into Charlotte's private quarters.

He hurried down the hall, wishing he had time to seek out a weapon. Surely Charles still held his collection of hunting rifles, even though he had ceased such activities years before. Another set of screams—these slightly more frantic—confirmed that York had no time for such a search.

He found the door in tatters, long splinters of wood covering the floor. Stepping into the room, he found Ahset standing over a kneeling Charlotte. The mummy's hands were wrapped tightly about the woman's throat and York knew that Charlotte's life span now numbered in the seconds.

York rushed forward and clenched both his hands together. He raised them over his head and brought down the two-handed blow with all his strength, striking Ahset on the back of her head. If it hurt her, she gave no indication other than a snarl of anger. York reached forward to seize Ahset's wrists, hoping to pull her hands off Charlotte's neck. As soon as he touched her skin, however, something strange occurred. He opened his mouth to scream but no sound emerged. What he sensed was terrible and profound. He literally felt the ending of Charlotte's life. He felt the fearful pounding of her heart and the gasping of her breath. He felt the exact moment when her life ended, and he shuddered as that final burst of energy flooded from her thrashing body into that of her killer. Ahset was literally feeding off Charlotte's death, and a portion of this power had transferred itself to York.

Finally able to yank himself away, York staggered back, panting heavily. He felt exhausted but euphoric, much like he would after lovemaking.

Ahset released Charlotte, letting the woman's dead body fall to the floor. She turned her intense gaze upon York and she smiled. "Did you like that?"

"No… it was horrible."

"I know the truth, Thomas. I was once just like you. The thought of taking another's life was frightening. But it gets easier—especially when you know the pleasure it can bring. It can make you powerful and keep you young. The essence of life is one of the most primal forces in the universe. And if you know how to tap into it and manipulate it, there is nothing that cannot be accomplished!"

York felt sweat dripping from his forehead. His temperature was spiking and he found it hard to slow the pounding his heart. "What's happening to me?"

"Your body is struggling to control the power it has received. I should be angry with you... that meal should have rightfully been mine." Ahset took several quick steps towards him, seizing his face in her hands. "I've never shared that moment with anyone before. I found it... strangely exciting."

Before York could respond, her lips found his. Her mouth was insistent and hungry...and York found himself returning her ardent attention. His mind swam as the life essence ran through his veins. Ahset pulled him towards the bed and they fell upon it, lost in the awful, dreadful moment.

They made love as Charlotte's corpse lay on the floor, mere feet away from them. The touch of Ahset's flesh, the feeling of power that ran through his body...it all swirled together in a heady mix that made York forget all of his doubts.

She was amazing.

~ ~ ~

Bulky and foreboding in the thick night fog, the steamship Stoker loomed over the pier to which she was moored, where busy ship's hands were loading the last pieces of cargo into her hold.

The dim lights cast from the pier were kind to the Stoker, hiding the scratched and unpainted hull of the ship. In fact, the lighting combined with the fog to give the false impression of grandeur to the steamship, making it appear to be a mammoth, proud vessel, when in fact it was rated at only eight thousand tons.

Though a freighter, the Stoker carried passengers, sometimes as many as two dozen. One of those passengers stood on the main deck, watching the men work. A stiff wind was blowing, but Thomas York was bundled up tight, with his hands stuffed deep into the pockets of his coat. The freighter would soon be leaving England, taking them on a lengthy voyage to the United States. It would be a chance to start anew, and York was anxious to be underway. He would carry the memory of his friend Charles for the rest of his life, but he wanted to be far away from the Sellas Estate.

"Mr. York?"

York looked to the side, where a young man with ruddy cheeks was staring at him expectantly. He was one of the junior crewmembers, off on his very first voyage. York had chatted amiably with him earlier in the day, soon after coming onboard. "Sammy, right?"

"That's right, sir." Sammy licked his lips in anticipation. "You mentioned that you might have a job that needed doing?"

"In exchange for a bit of money on the side?" York smiled warmly, letting Sammy know that he didn't mind being approached like this. "I do. I have a heavy case in my room that I need unpacked. Unfortunately, I injured my back during an altercation a few weeks ago and it hurts like bloody fire when I bend over."

Sammy blinked in surprise. "An altercation? Can't say I imagine a gentleman like you would be getting into scraps very often."

"You'd be surprised." York gestured for Sammy to follow him and together they passed into the bowels of the ship. Traveling on a vessel like this was far from glamorous. It was noisy and it smelled. Sammy was still so new that York could see his nose wrinkling at the scent of sweat and oil that filled the air.

Sammy cleared his throat as they approached the door to York's cabin. "Uh, sir?"

"Yes?"

"I don't mean to insult you but…"

York stopped with his hand on the handle of the door. "Out with it."

"I'm just here to unpack a box. Right?"

York stared at him for a moment before he realized what Sammy was asking. "Oh!" He laughed and nodded. "I'm not going to make a grab for your johnson, I assure you."

Sammy looked both embarrassed and relieved. "Had to ask. You hear lots of stories."

"Is this your first time away from home?"

Sammy nodded. "That obvious?"

"You told me you had just joined the crew but I figured you'd been on your own for a while."

Sammy shrugged. "Everyone has to leave the nest sometime."

"Right you are." York opened the door and ushered the young man inside. The cramped room was made even more so by the presence of a large object that stood against the wall. The sight of it made Sammy gasp.

"Is that…?"

York nodded, moving forward to run his hands over its surface. "It's a sarcophagus."

"Is there a mummy in there?"

"There is."

Sammy shook his head. "Are you taking it to a museum or something?"

"No. It's far too valuable to leave in the hands of academics."

Sammy grinned, enjoying the adventure of it. He looked around at the bags scattered around on the floor. "So what do you want me to help you with?"

"It's right here." York patted the sarcophagus. "The lid has a tendency to stick, and I need help to get it open."

"What do you need it open for?"

York sighed. "Sammy, I like you, but you're here to do a job. Will you help or not?"

Sammy looked chastened as he moved forward. He seized hold of the lid and strained, the veins popping out on his forehead. The lid was heavy and it was stuck, just like the gentleman had said. It opened with a sudden whoosh of air and Sammy stumbled back. He would have likely fallen had York not caught him and propped him up.

"Thank you, sir," Sammy murmured, pulling away. For the first time, he saw what lay inside the sarcophagus and he was so intrigued that he barely heard York's response. "Who is that?" he asked, his eyes widening as he saw a lovely young woman standing within the sarcophagus.

Ahset wore a sheath dress known as a kalasiris and it was form-fitting, accentuating every curve. It was held up by two straps, and it revealed the upper swells of her milky-white breasts but stopped just short of revealing anything more scandalous. In fact, it went all the way to her ankles, which was more than could be said for some of the gowns routinely worn by girls these days. Her naturally luxurious hair was enhanced by small extensions made of woven human and horse hair, while small ornaments hung from the tips.

"Her name is Ahset," York said. "Isn't she lovely?"

"She's the prettiest woman I've ever seen," Sammy said in amazement.

It was at that moment that Ahset opened her eyes and smiled.

York turned away as the mummy lunged for Sammy. He made sure the door was shut tight, knowing that the young man's screams would not be heard over the noises of the ship preparing for travel. He was so new to the crew that he might not even be missed for a few days and by that time, his corpse would have been thrown overboard. It was a disgusting thing to be a part of...but York was bound to the task now. He belonged to her.

"Share with me," Ahset whispered.

York turned back toward her and reached out with one trembling hand.

Together they dined.

TO RISE AND CONQUER

by Teel James Glenn

I.

Desperate, tired and hungry, the others kept saying it was hopeless, that the Japanese would find us and kill us in horrible ways. But I'm from Brooklyn: we don't do hopeless in Flatbush.

We'd escaped from the transport column three days ago, stolen a truck and headed due west toward Outer Mongolia in hopes of finding some guerrillas or members of the regular Chinese army. The truck all but rattled apart by the time it ran out of gas, and we had to hoof it. We hid the junker in a ravine and pushed on into the rough country.

There were six of us then.

Within hours of each other, Mister Kang and Lady Chung had dropped from exhaustion and the sicknesses the Japanese monsters had infected them with on the second night. At least they died free.

Now we were four: Doctor Jin Wu, his daughter Lily and a Japanese corporal, Hiro Yagyu. Me they call Gunner Hawkins. Oh, the birth certificate says Gerald Michael Hawkins, but I only heard that when my mom was angry at me. Everyone called me Gunner since an unfortunate incident with a potato gun at Newark Airport when I was six.

I spoke Mandarin passably, and no Japanese, but fortunately

the other three spoke varying degrees of English so we could communicate.

"I am afraid I cannot keep on like this," Doctor Wu said as the sun's rays began to go orange and the shadows lengthened. "I am slowing you down. You must leave me and take Lily."

"No, Father," the petite girl said. "I will not leave you." Her chao sam was torn and filthy, her hair in disarray, but she still had a grace and beauty about her that was above and beyond many another woman. It had been enough, along with her sweet personality, to cause Hiro to face disgrace and certain death by helping us escape and deserting his unit.

"Nobody is leaving anybody," I said in Chinese. "We are in this together."

"But they will catch up to us," the old man said. He had scholar's hands and bushy white eyebrows that shadowed his piercing eyes. "I am old and can only slow you down. I am useless. You must go on."

"No, Little Father," the Japanese soldier said. "You are not useless. You are a healer and have much wisdom. You and Lily will go with the American. I will stay to delay Captain Toshiro's squad." His voice was soft but with iron beneath it, the voice of someone who had spent his life bending to authority and, because his heart was captured by a pretty face, had turned and dug his heels in.

"Hiro!" Lily said with a gasp. It was clear from her expression that the Japanese turncoat had not fallen to Cupid's arrows alone.

"Easy, kids," I said. "Nobody is staying behind." I sounded older than Wu, but I was only a couple of years older than the two lovers, albeit hard years spent fighting–first to leave the streets of Brooklyn, then against the fascists in Spain and the Sons of the Rising Sun in Manchuria. "But we have to get out of this chill tonight and rest or we won't have any starch in the morning at all."

The country we were in had gone from gentle rolling hills to a veritable maze of broken ravines, which meant our progress had slowed as we were forced to zig-zag constantly. It also meant that those following us were slowed down as well.

It was arid and rocky and relatively flat, so I had to climb to the top of one of the ridges to get the lay of the land. Looking back the way we'd come I didn't see anyone, but I knew the Japanese patrol lead by Captain Toshiro was out there. I'd seen them earlier in the day, distantly against a grey sky, a column of men on foot. They were a full day behind us but with that martinet officer pushing them and our depleted condition that lead would soon disappear.

I looked down at the other three.

The Japanese kid was in over his head, a city kid pulled into the draft and sent to the wilds of Manchuria, exposed to cruelty he had never even imagined existed. He sat uncomfortably by Lily while she held her father's hand and tried to comfort him.

It would take a miracle for us to stay ahead of the thugs, but then I'd been living on miracles for quite a while—first in Spain, and then when Charlie Chennault said he needed pilots in China. I came to see what the Japanese had done to a proud, noble people. Three years and I'd come to love those people and their ancient land, feeling oddly enough as if I had come home. I'd often rounded a corner in some village and had that strange feeling of déjà vu, as if I had been there before. It had happened so frequently it was almost commonplace to me now.

"Can you see them?" Lily called up to me.

"Not at the moment, but they're out there," I said. Then, realizing how dark that sounded, I added, "We may have given them the slip."

It was all blarney, since I had little or no confidence we could get away from the relentless pursuit. We had no particular place to go, only the vague rumor of a Chinese army unit to the west. But I wasn't going down without a fight, and as tired and hungry as I was, I wouldn't offer much of that. And certainly the others wouldn't. We needed to rest and get out of the cold that darkness would bring.

Just then, as the last rays of the setting sun sliced across a ravine ahead of us, I got my miracle.

"Just a little further, folks," I said in as cheery a voice as I could muster as I jumped down to the others. "I just spotted a place to rest a little ways ahead."

It turned out to be a longer walk than I had guessed, but fifteen minutes later, stumbling in the dark we found the cleft in the side of the earth that I'd seen.

"It looked pretty deep," I said as I tore a strip from my ragged shirt and wrapped it around a broken tree branch to make a torch. "The sun hit it just right to see in. We can hide in there and I can pull these bushes over the opening."

Hiro had matches and he lit my makeshift torch that I then pushed into the opening. Inside was even bigger than it had seemed, more than deep enough for all four of us to tuck into.

"It goes back far enough so we can build a fire in here," Lily said. "It will not be seen from outside if we make it in that corner."

She helped her father in with Hiro moving ahead with my torch to find a place for him to sit comfortably.

"Look, there is water!" The Japanese called.

Sure enough, there was a little drip of water in one corner of the large space. It bubbled out from a crevice in the rock and formed a small pool the size of a large bowl before seeping into the ground. I tasted it.

"Good," I said. "This miracle just got better. See? Destiny can work for you!" I turned to the soldier. "Let's get some firewood."

I went outside with Hiro and we were able to gather two full armloads of dry brush quickly.

"Gunner-sama," he said as we headed back to the cave. "I fear we are merely delaying what will come."

I looked at him in the faint starlight and saw him for what he really was—not a soldier but a kid barely out of high school who was thrown into a violent world he had no heart for. He was scared and confused, but there was still something in him, some steel in his spine that had allowed his conscience to overcome his lifetime of drone-like upbringing.

"Life is about delaying what will come, kid," I said. "I think we got a good chance of staying out of Toshiro's way, especially now that we found that cave." I gave him my best fake smile. "Now you get in there and get a fire going for that pretty gal. I'll drop my pile here, get a bit more, then pull the bushes over the opening to hide us. Don't worry."

He nodded. I wasn't sure if he believed my pep talk or not, but he would keep up a front for Lily.

When he'd gone into the cave, I set down my sticks and picked up a leafy branch to walk back up the gully for a good distance the way we'd come. I climbed up on the side of the ravine again and looked back to the horizon.

I knew that somewhere out there were monsters in human form who would not rest until they killed all of us. I had the horrible feeling that I had used up my share of miracles and whatever destiny was waiting for me was not a good one.

I wish I'd known then that there were worse things in the world then the Sons of the Rising Sun and I was about to meet them.

II.

I stayed on that gully wall for a long time, straining my eyes for signs of the Kempeitai who were following us. I saw, or thought I saw, the phantom glow of a campfire in the far distance. I could only hope that they were as exhausted as we were and took a good long rest.

I really didn't have high hopes of finding either Mao's or Chang Kei Shek's troops or any real help, but I was damned if I was gonna give up. And I sure as hell wasn't going to let the Japanese take me alive. I had seen the horror first-hand at the place the Japanese called The Epidemic and Water Purification Department of the Kwantung Army.

The name was a cover for a horror show where the Japanese and their German collaborators performed hideous experiments on innocent civilians. Deliberate infections with smallpox, anthrax, and other diseases, test subjects for poisons, prisoners frozen till near death, starved, left untreated for terrible wounds, then vivisected—cut up while alive and without any anesthetic for "data." Even infants.

34

The Japanese military considered all races beside their own as subhuman. Worst of all, they seemed to have a particular hate for the Chinese.

They had invaded Manchuria in 1931 after they manufactured the Muken incident under the pretense of "aiding" the government, and had been raping the country and the people since then. The experimental station was just the most extreme example of their cruelty.

It was what had turned Hiro's stomach as well, and when he saw Lily and realized what would happen to her and her father he had rebelled.

I tore myself away from my pointless observations and set about erasing our footsteps with my branch. I felt like Tom Mix trying to hide from the Indians, but even with little faith in my "plan," I had to keep at it. I had to do something or I'd go a little mad with fear.

I had been held for two days in the main camp, and in those two days I had witnessed such horror—images of things I wanted to forget and probably never would be able to.

The irony of my capture by the Japanese was that I wasn't flying a combat mission against them when my plane's engine kicked out. I was carrying mail, including a letter to Charlie who had gone to Washington to try and get some unofficial U.S. help for China. He had a crazy idea that FDR would do something like a lend-lease with an air force. I'd burned the mail when I crashed, which ticked off the commander of the camp, their army's secret police number one boy, Captain Obata Toshiro.

From the first minute he set eyes on me, Toshiro made it his business to let me know my life under his care was going to be short and painful.

He knew I'd been flying against the Japanese, so no prisoner of war status for me. I was lowest of the low—a mercenary. So they sent me to hell on earth at the satellite camp to be used as a guinea pig. That meant a couple of days in a truck, packed like animals off to slaughter, twenty of us, mostly Chinese peasants whose lives had always been drudgery and were beaten down before the conquerors from Japan.

Among the packed human misery were the old college professor and his daughter, Lily. Hiro was the guard assigned to our truck.

I saw what was happening between Hiro and Lily, even if his superiors were too blinded by Jingoism to see it. The newly assigned boy already had doubts about the bill of goods Tojo and his boys had been selling him. The knowledge of what might happen to Lily and her father when we reached the camp was an obvious weight on the kid.

It was not hard to convince Hiro to make his move when I jumped the driver one night after we had stopped to camp. I had to leave the driver alive or it would have been too much for the new rebel to absorb, but I gambled on us getting far enough before the bound guard could get word to reinforcements.

I lost.

A patrol with a radio found him less than half a day after we took off and had Toshiro on our trail.

I shook myself to chase away the image of what might happen if they caught up with us and headed back to the cave. I dragged the branch to wipe out our tracks and then pulled enough foliage over the entrance to hopefully conceal us from any casual observation.

In the cave the others had a small fire going, and the warming flames made the place almost cozy.

Doctor Wu was already curled up asleep against the far wall. Lily and Hiro were sitting, staring into the fire, holding hands. When I entered he looked up.

"Don't worry, kids," I said when I saw them look up, a little startled when I made my entrance. "All is good out there. I covered the entrance and I'm gonna sleep. You'll have some time to yourselves."

I couldn't see them blush in the flickering fire shadows, but I would have bet they went beet red. I made my way to a little fold in the cave wall that blocked a direct line of sight to them but was still close to the fire and settled down to try and nap.

Didn't have to try hard. The second I put my back against the cave wall I was out like a light.

The next thing I knew, there was daylight streaming in from the brushy door. The fire was out, and the two lovers were wrapped around each other and looking like the kids they were—innocent and very, very young in their sleep.

Dr. Wu was sitting up, calmly looking out from the entrance. He smiled back at me when I moved over to sit beside him.

"You slept well?" he asked quietly.

"Better than I should have on solid rock," I said. "Anything going on out there?"

"No," he said, "It is quiet. Peaceful."

"At least they are," I said., indicating the sleeping kids.

His smile was a sage one. "Yes, the young have hope."

"You don't?"

"You are older than your years, Mister Hawkins," he said. "You know that we are but prolonging our hours. The invaders will never stop looking for us."

"Isn't that what we do every day, just prolong the days as long as we can?"

"Just so, but—"

"No 'but,' sir," I said. "If they catch us they catch us, but I will not stop for a moment thinking we can push on. Every minute they spend hunting us means they are not abusing someone else. Every tank of gas they use, every bit of food they use chasing us means we are costing them. So if they do get me, I will make them pay for the privilege every way I can."

The old man put a frail hand on my shoulder. "You Americans really all are still fighting the Alamo, are you not, my friend?"

"It may seem like that, Mister Wu," I answered with a laugh,. "but we don't like to lose. And, I guess in the end, those guys didn't really lose. They stopped the Mexicans. But I think we got a chance. We can hole up in here for the day, get our strength back and head out at night. We will find—"

"Papa!" Lily called from deep in the cave, "Come here!"

Both of us moved quickly into the cave to see that Lily and Hiro were at the back of the space, but partially hidden by a fold in the stone.

"What is it, daughter?"

"There is an opening back here."

Sure enough the two kids were standing at a cleft in the rock that was more than just another fold in the stone. Hiro held a match up and the yellow flare and showed a dark hole.

"That is carved out," Hiro said. He pointed to the edge of the opening. It clearly had been chiseled out of the naked rock. It looked also like there were cut steps further in the dark space.

The match went out.

"What do you think is in there?" Lily asked.

"I don't know," I called as I tore more of my shirt up and improvised a torch, "but we should see."

Hiro lit the cloth and I thrust the flame into the space.

There were stairs that went down to some sort of room. I started to move forward.

"Is it wise to take such a risk?" Dr. Wu asked me.

"Best to know if we have neighbors, Doctor," I said. "And who knows? Could be something down here we can use." Even as I spoke, I had a strange chill run up my spine, but I shrugged it off as childish squeamishness. Little did I know it was more. Much, much more.

III.

The stairs went down ten steps. Along the way, the rough wall of the cave became smooth and finished with symbols carved into it, so that by the time we reached the bottom, we knew we were standing in a man-made chamber.

"This is incredible," Doctor Wu said in a reverent tone. "These glyphs are ancient. Very ancient." He ran his fingers along the carved images while he leaned in to study them.

A few feet beyond, I could see what was clearly a door of some sort, the edges of the rectangle still crisp despite the obvious age of it all. On the center of the stone portal was the carved image of a herd of horses.

I felt an overwhelming sense of both familiarity and, oddly enough, horror at the sight of the door. I reached out and touched it.

"This is some sort of tomb," the old Chinese said. "A very old one. This is a warning or curse to keep all from violating it."

I felt a tingling in my fingers as they contacted the cool stone.

I was suddenly a little dizzy. The flickering of the torchlight seemed to imbue the figures on the door with real life, and I had the impression that I was looking out over a vast plain with herds of small, squat ponies racing in a cloud of dust.

"We had best to leave this place.," Hiro's voice suddenly drew me back from the strange vision. I shook myself and turned away from the door to see the others. Lily was hugging the soldier. "It does not feel right."

"Yeah," I said trying not to sound spooked. "Let's go back up. Nothing here we can use."

We went back up into the cave and I could see it wasn't just me who had had the eerie feeling down below, though I didn't dare ask them if they had a "vision" like I had.

The sun was well up outside the cave and I slipped out to look around. I saw no sign of anyone or anything, but found a scraggly bush with some berries on it, so I ate my fill and then grabbed as many as I could hold in an improvised pouch made from what was left of my shirt.

"Wonderful!" Doctor Wu exclaimed when he saw my haul. "These are most nutritious."

We all enjoyed the feast with some cool water, and for few moments were just four people having a picnic. The two kids even laughed and the doctor occupied himself with a stick in the dirt of the floor, recreating the symbols he'd seen below and pondering them. Me, I ran some memories at Ebbets Field across the movie screen of my mind and tried not to think about those guys out there somewhere looking for us.

After a bit, with our bellies full, we laid down to rest till nightfall when we planned to be on our way.

I should have slept like a baby with a full gullet and a solid place to rest, but I didn't.

The moment I closed my eyes I was gone again into that odd vision, only this time it was all-encompassing. I was overwhelmed by the smell and sight of the herd, the sound of their unshod hooves like thunder. I could not only hear the sound of the racing horses, but feel the vibrations of their myriad hooves rattling my teeth as they flowed across the barren open grasslands.

I felt my pulse race with them, then knew I was on one of them, flying across the ground. I had the sensation of leading others on horseback and looked back to see an army riding with me, men in silk shirts, laminated armor and helmets, shouting with savage joy.

The blood pumped in my veins, I found myself shouting back at them, urging them on. I was aware, somehow that they were my men, my followers. The very thought filled me with pride and power and something more—a sense of responsibility. To lead them was a burden as well as an honor, and I felt weary from that.

In the midst of the thrill of the running horses, there was the vision of blood and death, of horror and screams, cities burning, carnage on a grand scale, and it was as if I felt my own life leaving me, bleeding out of a thousand wounds. Above the pounding hooves I heard the screams of pain, the calls for mercy, and I felt my chest tighten.

Then I saw the women and children at the Japanese camp and heard them scream.

Abruptly I heard a jarring sound, a voice in a language I did not understand and I was awake, startled to be lying on the floor of that cave. It was strange to be in my own skin again and for a long moment I lie there breathing hard, a sense of fear shivering through my whole form.

What the hell? I thought, and then realized the guttural voice I had heard was speaking in Japanese. I looked over to see that Hiro and Lily were still asleep, nestled in each other's arms.

The voice was coming from outside the cave!

I scrambled to the entrance and was horrified to see that a Japanese patrol was right outside the cave. I didn't wait to see how many there were, but moved back quickly to wake the others.

"Shh!" I hissed and, hand over each mouth to quiet them, made everyone aware of our plight. I pointed toward the back of the cave and they all took the hint and headed back, quietly, to the hidden stairs.

I spent a few moments to disguise the remains of our fire so that anyone looking casually into the cave could not tell it had been recently occupied, then followed the others into the dark lower chamber.

Due to a peculiarity of the stone, we could clearly hear the troopers outside the cave opening as clearly as if they were standing next to us—better, in fact, than we had upstairs in the main cave.

"Do they know we are here?" Lily asked.

"I don't think so," I whispered.

"No," Hiro said. "They do not. The officer is ordering his men to set up camp before nightfall. They are waiting for a detachment that has fallen behind them. That one is being led by Captain Toshiro."

Upstairs the sounds of the soldiers grew and there was a change in the tone.

"What is it, Hiro?"

"One of the men has discovered the entrance to the cave," he said. "They are entering."

I couldn't see a thing in the dark, but the tremor in his voice told me all I needed to visualize the fright on his features.

I felt the carved stone of the door behind my back and reached a hand to run it along the raised haunches of the horses on it. Again I felt the tingling through my fingers that ran up my arm this time and charged my entire body. As if guided by some unseen force my fingers found a projection on the door and I pressed against it.

There was a click and a portal opened so abruptly that I all but fell back into the space with an exclamation.

"What has happened?" Doctor Wu asked at my startled cry.

"I found a way into the tomb," I said. "Quickly, come in." The others followed, each of us holding onto each other's hands to stay together.

"I can see you, Hiro" Lily said.

She was right; there was a bluish light that suffused the space.

41

It seemed to come from all around us, emanating from the walls. It was enough for me to make out the rectangle of the doorway we had come through and the vague shapes of my companions. I could also see other silhouettes in the space as my eyes became accustomed to the pale illumination.

Instead of the musty smell one would expect of the room, I smelled flowers, spices and wild places, the smell of the steppes.

Above us the sound of the soldiers was louder and in defense against discovery, I pushed the stone door closed after us.

When the door was closed tight, the light within the space brightened and I could see what the shapes in the room with us were.

The size of the chamber became clearer in the strange blue light now—a long rectangle ten feet on one side and twenty-five or more on the other, with a vaulting ceiling several feet above our heads. The walls were hung with what looked like tapestries that had images on them, though in the faint light it was hard to see what they might depict.

At the other end of the room from us, on a raised pedestal, was the most unusual thing I had ever seen. Under a cloth canopy held up by four spears was what appeared to be a throne.

I found myself compelled to slowly walk toward the other end of the room. It was as if some force was pulling me across the space. The others followed me and the four of us approached the throne holding our breaths.

Flanked by two terra cotta horses, on that throne was seated a fantastic figure.

Even in the dim light I could see that the figure was attired in rich fabrics, a long robe and laminate armor with a small furred hat atop his head. What was most startling about the apparition, however, was that it was not a statue. It was a mummified human figure!

I had to touch it.

I reached out my fingers to the armor. It was dusty and dry, but it did not crumble at my touch. I moved my hand up to the face. It was textured fabric but surprisingly not brittle nor like old leather.

It felt supple.

"Give me a match, Hiro," I whispered.

I lit the match and the orange flame revealed first tufts of red hair peaking from beneath the fur hat and then the whole face of the figure. It was a proud, wide cheek-boned visage that was discernable through the layers of fine cloth that had been used to preserve the flesh of the individual. Most startling of all was the figure's wide-open eyes. They were green, and they reflected the light of the match. They seemed to shine with a lambent light of their own, almost as if the presence of the man behind them still burned within the mummified shell.

Lily gasped.

"This was a notable man," Doctor Wu said softly. "Certainly some minor chief. What I read on the wall before made me suspect it, but this confirms it."

I barely heard him as the contact with the wrapping on the corpse sent a bolt of sensation through me, an icy chill and a heat at once. I do not know how I knew, but at that moment my knowledge was sure and absolute.

"No, Doctor Wu," I said. "This was not some minor chief. This was the chief of chiefs, the Great Khan. This was, this is…Genghis Khan himself!"

IV.

"The Great Khan?" Doctor Wu said with shock. "By what knowledge do you make such a claim?"

"I don't know," I said, "but it is him." I couldn't keep from staring into the eyes of the mummy. Even after the match went out I felt them glaring at me, accusing me. They seemed to say "Bow down before me in my tomb."

"It could be so, Father," Lily spoke up. "The stories say his tomb has never been found."

"But daughter, would it not be grander than this?"

"No," I said. I didn't know how I knew it, but I did. "He was a simple nomad chief, after all was said and done. A regular Joe, so to speak. He wouldn't have wanted much. I'll bet those hangings tell the story of his life. And see, he has two spirit horses beside him and a sword at his side. What else could a nomad warrior want in the next world?"

"And a simple tomb would be easy to conceal in its day," the Doctor said.

I looked all around us in the almost cozy room, and then realized we were walking on rugs. The whole feeling of the space, I realized now, was of a yurt. I was sure that if we were to examine the rest of the space, we would find eating utensils, bowls and the everyday things of a horseman's kit.

Hiro moved to reach for the sword on the mummy's hip.

"No," I said, "let's not touch anything. This is a holy site."

"Just so," Doctor Wu said. "We will leave as soon as we can." He gave a deep bow before the seated mummy and I found myself joining him. Hiro and Lily both followed suit.

The Japanese boy lit another match, and the visage from the past regarded us again with stern eyes.

Once more the green eyes stared back at us with a fierceness in death that could only make me wonder how powerful they must have been in life.

Whether from our movement or some other reason, the head of the mummy shifted ever so slightly then, the effect being that it appeared to be turning a bit to look directly at us. It was so startling that Lily took a step back, and in doing so tripped. She let out an involuntary yell.

Hiro jumped to catch her but the damage was done, the same anomaly that amplified the sound from above carried her cry to the Japanese outside the tomb door.

"Damn!" I cursed. I turned just in time to see the door to the space pushed in and be blinded by a flashlight beam.

"Teishi!" A Japanese soldier yelled. "Kofuku!"

"He says to surrender," Hiro said with defeat in his voice, yet he

44

stood tall and stepped in front of Lily. "We are dead."

There was much shouting after that and the room was filled with Japanese soldiers who were rough about forcing us out at bayonet point. Behind us I could hear them ransacking the space, though whether they were looking for others or just being jerks I couldn't tell.

"I wouldn't do that, guys," I said as I was shoved into the corridor, "I don't think the owner will like it." I got a rifle butt to my kidney for my trouble.

They brought the four of us out of the cave and threw us roughly to our knees in front of the little tin god of the Kempeitai, Captain Obata Toshiro. He was taller than most of his men, almost as tall as me, and uncharacteristically barrel-chested for a Japanese.

He stood with legs spread, hands on hips and a broad smile on his angular face. "You think you are so smart, American," he said with his perfect California accent, courtesy of three years at UCLA. "But who is the smart one who will pay now?"

"I don't know, Obata, " I said, really unable to control my smart mouth. "Seems to me when word gets back to your bosses that you let a bunch of prisoners make a monkey out of you, you're the one who's gonna pay."

That did nothing to endear me to him and he stepped forward calmly and backhanded me across the face. The shock of the blow sent me flat to the ground and brought the bitter taste of blood into my mouth. I grinned.

"Struck a nerve, eh, Toshiro?" I spat out. He moved to kick me but the arrival of one of his troopers stopped him. The man came running up and bowed, then presented him with the sword in its scabbard from the tomb.

The short sword's sheath was jewel-encrusted, and the Japanese officer held it up so the gems caught in the firelight and sparkled.

"Oh so," Toshiro said. "Kirei!" He drew the single edged, curved blade and sliced the air with it. Then he turned his attention back to me.

"You see, American," Toshiro said, "You have even brought me treasure from this filthy country of animals." He swung the sword with the practiced ease of someone familiar with a katana. "I think it will even be useful." He gave an order in Japanese and Hiro was dragged up to his knees, arms held out to the side. Toshiro raised the blade above his head.

"You have brought disgrace to your family and your emperor," Toshiro said. "You deserve no consideration."

Hiro was tight-lipped and stoic as he stared up at his superior.

Lily began to cry hysterically.

"Do not cry, Lily," Hiro said with steel in his tone. "We will be together in the next life."

I stared at the upraised sword, felt a chill shoot through me and suddenly my vision of the horses on the grassland returned to fill my mind. Cries of exultation and triumph flooded into me and I felt a surge of power unlike any I had ever felt. It propelled my legs to spring me forward so that I collided with Toshiro's legs and sent him toppling.

The officer cursed in Japanese and kicked me solidly to the side of my head, sending me flying and seeing stars. The pounding in my head was the thunder of horses' hooves again, and the stars that danced before my eyes were the glints of sunlight off of armored bodies.

The vision overlaid the Japanese cursing and the figures of the soldiers racing to grab me and pull me roughly to my feet.

Toshiro stood before me his face a mask of hate. "You dare to lay your filthy hands on a servant of the emperor?" He hauled off and slapped me back to my knees and his men picked me up again.

"If I'd gotten my hands on your skinny neck, we wouldn't be having this conversation," I managed to spit out. All I could taste was blood and I still couldn't hear clearly, but I didn't need a translator for the cascade of obscenities he vomited at me while using me for a punching bag.

The pain was intense, but I reached the point where I began to— or perhaps continued to—hallucinate. The images in front of me were no longer a bunch of Sons of the Rising Sun. Instead, I was looking at great herds of horses again, but this time cavalry charged into the midst of the herd, small men in armor waving curved swords and calling to me.

The world spun into darkness then, and I knew nothing until I swam up from the pit of unconsciousness to see Hiro before me. The Japanese boy's face was swollen and bloody, his right eye all but closed, but he was staring at me with great intensity.

"Gunnar-sama," he whispered with great relief in his voice. "I was afraid you were dead."

I felt as if I was. Every part of my body hurt. I tried to make sense of what was happening and came to realize I was on my side facing Hiro. He must have seen the confusion on my face because he continued speaking.

"Captain Toshiro was furious, and I was afraid he had beaten you to death. But you saved my life, Gunnar-sama. He left me to attack you. He said he would make us both suffer later."

"I'm sure he will," I managed to croak. My throat was dry and I could taste blood.

"I thank you." The boy's tone was almost religious and I felt a little embarrassed by his gratitude.

"I'm afraid it was just a sleight reprieve, Hiro, but any time is good time if you use it right." Suiting action to words, I started to work at the ropes that held my arms and legs but it did nothing but make me more sore and start to depress me. It really looked like this Flatbush kid's number was finally up.

V.

I stopped struggling out of exhaustion and was aware for the first time that quite a bit of time had passed since my encounter with Toshiro. The Japanese camp was asleep, the cook fire burnt low and a false dawn already pinking the horizon.

I could see Lily and her father, bound painfully like Hiro and I were and sleeping fitfully near us. Toshiro had a tent set in the center of the encampment, a luxury he had his men carry for him. It had a banner proclaiming his Samurai heritage on it, and it looked like something out of old woodcuts.

"Bet he snores," I said aloud.

"What?" Hiro whispered.

"Never mind," I said. "I'm just using up the last of my words. I don't expect to get much chance in not too long."

"Then you accept that we will soon be dead?" There was no fear in his voice, and I felt an odd sense of pride in the kid. He had grown up a lot in the last few days. "It is good to die with honor."

"I don't think honor or not will matter once we shuffle off this mortal coil," I said. But as I said it I realized I was just a little angry that it really had come to that. And I felt helpless, a feeling I didn't like.

I looked away from Hiro to beyond the dozing guards watching over us where I could see the two dozen Japanese soldiers huddled under blankets. Some of them, I noticed, slept under the plundered tapestries from the tomb. I felt even angrier at seeing that. It was an anger that flared to full flame when Toshiro exited his tent.

The Japanese officer stood tall, as if posing for a portrait of arrogance personified. He had the sword stolen from the tomb hanging from his belt. He stretched and then looked to where we were bound. And he smiled.

That smile made me see a red haze and then the haze dissolved into something else, a blinding red mist that blocked all out before me and at that moment I was not seeing the sneering Toshiro or the troops. I was not seeing my fellow prisoners.

Instead, I saw before me the vision again of the mounted warriors in ancient garb and felt their anger channel through me. They chanted and roared and cheered, and I felt their cries flow though me like flaming energy, making me feel like the most powerful being in the world, capable of anything. I knew they were chanting my name, "Temujin," they called like the roar of a great cataract or an approaching tornado. "Temujin!"

Everything blurred before me again, and I was looking at the blue-lit interior of the tomb.

I tried to make sense of it all, but my confusion was not only my own and I knew it. I looked down to see hands before me. They were my hands and they were not. They were stubby-fingered hands, covered in loosely wrapped bandages. They were thrust out from silk robe sleeves. I could see before me the ransacked tomb, the terra-cotta horses shattered, the wall hangings torn down and taken.

I felt myself—that was not myself—rising and moving across the room toward the door. Footsteps, muffled by the carpet in the tomb, echoed as this other me moved across the room to the door and then up the stairs.

Suddenly a boot slammed into my side and I was on the ground again, looking up at a sneering Toshiro standing above me.

"Time to wake up, American," the officer said. His boot shocked me but there was a curious distance from any pain from it, as if my spirit was somewhere else. "It will be a lovely day as we march you back to your fate. We would not wish you to miss a glorious moment of it."

I looked up at his leering face and it was oddly out of focus, superimposed over the inner staircase on the way to the cave. The sounds were overlaid as well, the cold laugh of the officer with the muffled scream of one of the soldiers in the cave as the leathery hands of my other self wrapped around the startled Japanese's throat and squeezed.

"You have nothing to say, American?" Toshiro said. His expression became cross when I did not cower at his taunting. He turned his attention to Hiro and kicked him hard, speaking roughly in Japanese. The boy simply glared back at him in silence.

By now Lily and Mister Wu were awake, and the girl sobbed at the sight of her boyfriend abused. This drew the officer's attention and he turned from the boy to her.

"Perhaps you should help reward my men for their diligence," Toshiro said. "It will be a while till we can find some comfort women for them in this forsaken backwater of a country." He moved to the girl's side and reached down for her, which had its intended result in bringing a stream of profanity from Hiro.

The officer laughed and reached down to grope the girl and the boy squirmed in agony, which only made Toshiro laugh again.

I only heard the laugh as a distant echo over the gurgling death rattle of the soldier at the cave mouth. At the same time that I watched Toshiro abuse the girl to her screams of terror, I heard the yells of a soldier outside the cave mouth scream, "Yurei!"

Toshiro snapped his head around at the soldier's cry and I had the odd experience of seeing the officer through two sets of eyes, my own from the ground and my "other self" from the cave mouth.

The whole camp came awake now with a war camp's alertness, weapons jumping into hands as they took up defensive positions.

I watched it all unfold and heard it all from two vantage points on the ground and as my other self swept forward. I rolled over to watch the scene unfold before me like a nightmare in the morning light.

The tottering form of the Khan's mummy from within the tomb moved forward in double exposure at the wakening soldiers, Ariska rifles leaping into their hands. The bolts all clicked back and the bullets exploded from them.

I felt the impact in my body like bee stings as I saw the bullets rip into the bandaged-wrapped figure of the mummy. They did not stop the moving figure—my moving figure—as the undead Khan lumbered straight to one of the nearest troopers.

Toshiro screamed at the top of his lungs, exhorting his men to attack.

Lily screamed as well, and the cacophony—repeated twice to my ears—was deafening. The bee stings continued, and my head rang and my anger rose as the bullets slammed into the duality that was Khan and me.

The mummy began to move with greater speed at each moment. As each bullet tore through the silk of its robes, small puffs of fabric exploded from him, yielding dust and skin but no blood.

And with each quickening step, the mummy seemed to find another trooper, the stubby fingers tearing at living flesh, rending human bone and limbs with the resulting gore splattering the whole of the ravine in crimson death.

Lily's voice was a steady siren of horror now. Toshiro's exhortations were vitriolic, and he waved the sword of the Khan like a bandleader's baton.

I was transfixed, watching myself in the nightmare of it all, moving with a warrior's muscle memory to bring death to each soldier who held his place. But some did not hold. Some of the Japanese troopers threw their weapons down and ran in terror.

I will say this for Toshiro: the little weasel had guts. He stood his ground and swung the sword at the approaching mummy with a fury that should have halved the nightmare, but Khan and I moved with now lightning speed and grabbed the sword arm at the wrist.

For a long moment the two stood, eyes locked, with the officer straining to free his hand from the vise grip of horror. Then, with seemingly no effort, the mummy tore Toshiro's right arm off at the shoulder.

The officer's scream cut off abruptly as his limb went flying, but not before the mummy had wrenched the sword from the now dead hand. When the Japanese dropped to his knees the mummy swung the sword to decapitate Toshiro with a single, clean stroke.

Abruptly all was silence in the ravaged camp, save for Lily's quiet sobbing. It was a deafening silence, made more so by the fact that I heard it twice over and saw myself and the mummy, each from the other's point of view. The emerald eyes of the undead thing stared down at me, and I knew then that the world was changed and I was part of it.

It was a mirror darkly tinged with blood, and I feared it would soon mingle with my own.

VI.

It was a frozen moment, looking up in the morning light at the bullet-riddled mummy, stained with fresh gore and with strips of fabric trailing from it.

Mister Wu was praying in Chinese, Hiro in Japanese, and Lily was sobbing, but I could find no words. Nor did I need them.

We saw each other, the mummy and I, with clear eyes and linked memories. The horses' hooves of long ago thundered louder than the echoes of the gunshots just moments earlier. I saw vast armies sweeping across the grasslands, felt the sweaty warmth of my horse beneath me, almost a part of me.

The words spoken were none that I knew, and yet I understood all of them. "Prisoner, son, husband, chief, Great Khan," I was all of them, but the ones I cherished most were, "comrade, brother, father."

The green eyes of the mummy burned into mine and then I saw him separate himself from me to look at the other prisoners with a keen intelligence behind them.

The mummy raised his sword over its head and I had a flash of my own life come to me, but instead of flinching I stared back at the horror and stretched my neck to make it easier for him.

"Do it, Karloff," I snarled, "At least I got to see these monkeys get theirs first."

The blade paused at the apex of the swing then flashed down between eye-blinks. The razor tip of the ancient sword sliced through my bounds and suddenly I was free.

The mummy turned from me and walked to the fallen form of Toshiro and tore the scabbard of the sword from the corpse. He then resheathed the blade and strapped it around its waist.

I rolled over and untied Hiro, who then went to Lily and her father and freed them both.

I stood on nearly numb legs, my whole body aching but kept my eyes on the horror that now was still in the center of the destruction it had caused. I was no longer linked directly to the figure, my vision singular again, but it was clear that he was looking out across the broken terrain, looking almost directly into the rising sun.

The golden rays sparkled off the ancient silks of the mummy and I had the sense of longing as his emerald eyes looked to the horizon. After a long moment the mummy turned to look at me, fixing me with his eyes. He pointed at the fallen Japanese then held out his hand in an expansive gesture to the countryside.

I knew what he was asking even without our connection.

"Yes," I said in Mandarin. "These are invaders. Lowlife monsters who are raping this country and killing its people in wholesale numbers."

The wrappings of the ancient warrior were not so thick that I could not read expression on his features. His brows narrowed and his eyes burned intensely green. He looked to Mister Wu, Lily and Hiro, around whom Lily had wrapped herself.

"It is as he says, Great Khan," the old Chinese said. "These dogs have come across the sea to destroy all that is good and right. The great dragon is beset with rabid dogs and I fear will succumb."

The mummy inclined his head, strands of red hair escaping the helmet to fall over his eyes.

"I'm afraid he's not exaggerating," I said. "These guys are just the tip of the iceberg."

The mummy waved a hand again at the distant countryside then clenched a fist in a gesture of "mine."

"Yes it was all yours, once," I said. "From here to the Mediterranean. Now Tojo and his boys want that, but not the government of religious tolerance you had."

The mummy removed his helmet then, the shock of red hair going to white visible through the wrappings on his head. He threw his head back and opened his mouth. The sound that issued forth from his desiccated lips was like nothing I had ever heard before, a deep two-tone sound that warbled from near the top of the scale to so deep it vibrated my diaphragm.

The strange sound reverberated off the walls of the ravine and crawled up across the land in all directions then echoed back to us strong enough to make the hairs on my neck stand up. The sound flowed over me in waves, stunning me and yet calling to me with a strange exotic quality I cannot describe.

It was a sound older than time, a compulsion stronger than death. It called to someplace deep within me, in the center of my being, and I knew it would call me to follow it even beyond the grave and it soon became clear that that was its job.

The ground around the camp, for a radius of two hundred yards from the cave where the Great Khan had slept, began to tremble. At first it felt like an earthquake but then I realized it was something else, something sinister and frightening. The earth began to undulate like the surface of a lake, a gentle rolling movement that soon grew staccato and spasmodic.

"What is happening?" Lily managed to gasp.

At first I was not sure myself, but then the first hand began to claw its way out of the hard clay of the Mongolian soil like a strange flower breaking through the topsoil. This was followed quickly by another and another, until there were several hundred desiccated figures crawling free from shallow graves all around us. They were all, or rather in life had all been, squat men with broad shoulders and stubby legs. They were dressed much like their leader was in silk shirts and laminate armor with helmets rusted with the red clay of the countryside to give them the aspects of stone men. All their black eyes were focused on the bandage-wrapped figure that had summoned them from their guardianship sleep.

Soon the mummy of the Great Khan stood in the circle of several hundred undead figures. The red-haired mummy turned then to look past his men to fix his lambent emerald eyes on me and spoke haltingly in Mandarin.

"This was country," he said. His voice was like dark music played on an instrument not meant to play it. "It will be my country again."

I looked at the others transfixed as I was by the green eyes of the Great Khan. Then his voice called me again, "I have seen your heart. I have known your mind. Join me."

For a moment I heard the thundering of a thousand horses' hooves again, but then realized it was, in fact, my own heart beating hard in my chest.

There were hundreds of thousands of Japanese with horrible weapons of death all across the country he called his own, and it seemed like it would be a hopeless thing to oppose them. But like I once said, I'm from Flatbush and I don't do hopeless.

I leaned down and scooped up a rifle from the corpse of one of the Japanese soldiers, aware that there would soon be many, many more just like it all the way to Tokyo.

"Okay, Genghi baby," I said. "Let's go kick Tojo's ass!"

THE WEIGHING OF THE DEAD

by Sam Gafford

Cairo, Egypt
1933

O n a small dirty street off of the main road, nearly hidden by boxes and debris, sat a tiny store that was overlooked by the casual observer.

The weathered sign above the door said only, "Curios," but everyone knew it was the shop of Sarenpet, procurer of thieves. It was the place to come to sell something that had been procured by nefarious means or, conversely, to arrange for something to be procured. Nefariously, of course.

On a hot summer day, with the sun nearly at its height, two men walked up and entered the store. One was a smaller, pale man with a slight hump on his back and hair gone gray from a lifetime of study. He wore a white suit, impeccably tailored with a wide Panama hat placed at precisely the right angle, and carried a heavy walking stick. The other man was darker and thicker both in muscle and thought. He wore loose, dark clothes despite the heat of an Egyptian afternoon. Both men appeared grim and determined. As the bell over the door rang with their entrance, the large man reached up and silenced it effortlessly, trying not to squash it in his hands.

The small man moved into the store and looked over the merchandise disdainfully. Much of it was covered in dust and grime. The "curios" here were nothing but junk, designed to trick tourists or simply fill out the shop. No one had bought any of them in years, and the small man gave them barely a glance.

"Sarenpet," he said firmly, "I am here."

From behind the curtain at the back of the store came the noise of someone shuffling forward. An old Egyptian peered out and then pushed the curtain aside. He looked warily at the two men, weighing a decision in his mind. Having made it, he finally walked forward.

"Dr. Greenwood," he said to the smaller man. "I was not expecting you. I'm sorry, but I have nothing for you."

Greenwood looked at the man. He had met many like him before in his years chasing artifacts and would doubtlessly meet many more. Sarenpet was a tiny man, made large and important purely through the money he could provide for goods or information.

Sighing, Dr. Greenwood began to put on his white gloves. He hated to get any part of his clothing dirty, but in Cairo, it was impossible to avoid it.

"You disappoint me, Sarenpet. After all this time, you still think that I cannot tell when you are lying."

The Egyptian sputtered in mock fury. "I never lie!"

"And even that is a lie. Matthew?"

The large man stepped forward and grabbed Sarenpet roughly. Holding the merchant from behind, he forced the Egyptian's right hand open on the counter. Sarenpet struggled but could not escape the muscle man's grip.

"It's useless to resist," Dr. Greenwood drawled as he tested the weight of his cane, "Matthew can hold you like that for hours before he tires. If time were a luxury, I would enjoy bantering and haggling the information out of you. But the hours grow short and I cannot spare a moment. Now, what have you learned about the Winslow Expedition?"

Sarenpet struggled harder, trying to get a grasp on Matthew behind him, but he was rewarded only with a painful squeeze from the strongman.

"Howard Carter," Sarenpet grunted, "had consulted with Winslow in 1924 during his lecture tour in New York City. Carter gave Winslow the location of what he thought was a lesser tomb of some priest of minor importance. Winslow went into the desert in 1926 and disappeared, never to be seen again."

Dr. Greenwood shook his head. "Yes, yes, yes. I know all that. But there was a box, the very last thing that Winslow sent out of the desert before he vanished. It came here. I know it came here, Sarenpet, because I have the thief who stole it and brought it to you. So now you are going to tell me what you did with it."

Sarenpet shook his head desperately. Sweat was falling down his face but not from the heat. "I cannot!" he pleaded.

Dr. Greenwood nodded at Matthew, and the silent strongman pressed down on Sarenpet's hand, spreading the fingers even further. Swiftly, with no hesitation, Greenwood brought the heavy head of his cane down fully on the little finger of Sarenpet's right hand. The Egyptian screamed horribly.

"You, you can't do this," he cried through tears of pain. "You're … you're a good man. I know the sect you serve. You're not supposed to harm people. Only help."

Dr. Greenwood smiled. "Why, my dear Sarenpet, whatever gave you the idea that I was one of the good guys? Is it because I wear a white hat? Where did the box go?"

The procurer of thieves whimpered but would not speak. His small finger looked as if it had been mangled in a press. Greenwood took careful aim at the index finger.

There was the sound of a cane smashing down onto a desk and a man's screams being muffled.

Outside, a dog pawed absentmindedly in the dust.

London, England
June 12, 1934

It was a summer morning like only London can produce—overcast, rainy and dreary.

Claire Montgomery quickly moved through the throngs of traffic with the experienced ease of a born New Yorker. Without a care or even a thought, she threaded her way through the cars which beeped almost apologetically, showing the usual British restraint. Claire was already late and the delay on the underground hadn't helped.

With the front gates of the London Museum finally in sight, she broke into a near sprint, closely avoiding several collisions with busy pedestrians. The outside of the building had several large placards announcing upcoming exhibits, but of course, all anyone wanted to talk about was Egypt.

Ever since Howard Carter had broken through the wall of King Tut's tomb in 1922, proclaiming that he could see "wonderful things" in the room beyond, the world had gone Egypt crazy. It was all anyone wanted to talk about, and suddenly, archeological experts in Ancient Egypt found themselves in great demand. The riches of King Tut's tomb had been removed and sent on exhibition across the globe, and Howard Carter had become the "thinking man's celebrity." Before finding that tomb, Carter would have had difficulty getting anyone to buy him a cup of coffee, much less finance an exhibition. Now the man traveled the world, giving lectures and pulling in large speaking fees.

And it wasn't just all about King Tut, either.

Every tomb in Egypt was now ripe for plunder, and virtually all of them had been. There were still a few here and there that managed to remain hidden, but most everyone believed that there would never be another find like King Tut. Still, the public was hungry for anything Egyptian, and museums were just as eager to cash in on the craze. A new Egyptian exhibit could translate into massive public relations gains as well as a great number of patron donations and ticket sales. No museum knew this better than London's prestigious British Museum.

Rushing down Great Russell Street, Claire turned and sprinted across the large court to the front doors. Even though it was barely nine a.m., there were plenty of people about. Moving through the great doors, she passed the sign which read: "FREE ADMISSION to all studious and curious persons." This had been the policy since the great museum had opened in 1759. The British Museum had become one of the most famous centers of learning and study in the world, and Claire still couldn't believe that she worked there. Now, if only her boss weren't a complete jerk, her life might actually be pretty good for a change.

She turned a corner and nearly ran into Arthur Peabody, one of the security guards. He smiled broadly and tipped his cap to her. Arthur was a little old and a little too paunchy to be an effective guard but he had been at the museum for nearly fifty years, so like an exhibit, they kept him on.

"Any new sightings of your phantom, Arthur?" Claire teased, already trying to hurry down the hallway.

"Now, you may well go ahead and laugh at old Peabody, Miss Montgomery, but I ain't laughing. I found another mess this morning, not too far from your boss' office, as a matter of fact."

This stopped her cold. Dr. Claude Titus, head of the museum's Egyptology Department and Claire's immediate supervisor, did not have much patience for anything that disrupted his routine or made a mess. Disruptions and messes were things that Claire tended to create more often than she wished, which meant her job hung by a thread that could snap very easily.

"What are you talking about, Arthur? What happened? Did Dr. Titus see it?"

Arthur smiled and shook his head. "Your fearless leader has been locked in his office all morning, talking to some other big-named fellow. He didn't see a thing."

Claire realized she was holding her breath in and let it out with a sigh. "That's good. What happened?"

"Oh, you know, the usual. A couple of boxes were overturned and emptied, stuff thrown on the floor. Near as I could tell, nothing was broken, so I just put them back in their crate and left the top off so you could take a look. I don't think anything was stolen. At least, I hope nothing was stolen."

"How many does this make now?"

"Well, let me think. I noticed the first one about eight months or so ago when they had that Chinese exhibit. You remember?" Claire nodded but could feel the clock ticking faster and faster. She needed to get down there and make sure nothing was missing or damaged.

"I guess, maybe, this is the ninth time I've found something. I'm telling you, Miss Montgomery, this place is haunted, and the ghost likes your area the best! It wouldn't surprise me if one of those mummies you got down there was cursed and is walking around at night."

Claire laughed. "I'm sure it's nothing like that. I'll check the box, Arthur. Thanks!" As quick as possible, she ran down the hall to the access stairway and descended into the bowels of the museum.

The main floor of any museum is like the top of an iceberg. The bulk of the beast lies below, unseen by most. The massive collections are stored in hundreds of bins, vaults and catacombs beneath the main floor. Many of those items are never even seen by the public. They are catalogued and either used for study or filed away—ironically, like mummies in tombs. No one, except maybe the director of the museum, knows exactly what is stored within the strangled maze of offices and halls and locked gates. So much is kept down there, Claire had once thought, that it would be so easy to lose something, or someone, in all of it.

Reaching the second floor from the bottom, Claire hurried through the access door and down through the maze of cabinets and shelves. As she neared the corner, she felt relief at the sight of Titus' closed door and the muffled sound of voices from inside. Quickly, she dropped her bags at her tiny, inadequate desk and began looking around for what Arthur had described to her. A few rows back, hidden behind another shelf, she found an old wooden box just sitting there with the cover open and set aside.

It was a shipping crate, one that had apparently been there for God knows how many years. It was addressed to the British Museum, but the return address was a shipping company in Cairo. Claire couldn't make out the name. Carefully, she felt around inside and pulled out a few items. She looked at them curiously. They were idols, or small statues, of various Egyptian gods. Despite being old, though, there was nothing especially remarkable about them. They were the types of things that would have been found in any Egyptian tomb, a sort of ancient bric-a-brac. Still, someone had considered them important enough to send to the British Museum, but Claire just couldn't figure out why.

"I'm telling you, Dr. Greenwood, there is nothing of the sort anywhere in the collection," Dr. Titus' voice boomed with self-importance as he escorted his guest out of the office.

The other man was smaller, with a slight hunch to his back. He wore an all-white suit. Claire couldn't stop herself from thinking that he looked like a fancy version of the Good Humor ice-cream man. It was clear that he was very impatient and had little tolerance for Titus.

"Dr. Titus," he said slowly, "I assure you, I am not mistaken. I have followed the trail from the desert to Cairo to Paris to New York and it has led here. You don't understand. These objects are extremely dangerous, and I must insist that you relinquish them at once."

Titus looked at the other man like he was looking at a bug.

"I know who you are, Dr. Greenwood, and I know your reputation. You fancy yourself some sort of expert in the occult and all that nonsense. Frankly, you're an embarrassment to men of science. I only agreed to this meeting because, for some reason, our director thinks well of you. Well, I've listened to you, and that's all I'm obligated to do. We don't have anything in the collection from any expedition headed up by this Winslow person and that's the end of it. Now, if you'll excuse me, I have real work to do."

Titus went back inside his office and shut his door. Dr. Greenwood glowered at the barrier, and as he turned to leave, saw Claire standing sheepishly by her desk. "Please excuse the scene, Miss...?"

"Montgomery," she answered. "Claire Montgomery. I'm Dr. Titus' assistant."

The little man bowed slightly. "Then you have my sympathy, Miss Montgomery. Your employer is, for lack of a better word, a fool."

She smiled and said, "Well, I'm afraid I can't comment on that, sir."

"Discreet and loyal. I admire that."

"Well, discreet at least."

Dr. Greenwood smiled. "And an American, from your accent?"

"Yes, sir. Born and raised in New York City."

"Wonderful city," Dr. Greenwood replied. "I've a house there near Central Park. Sadly, I do not visit there as much as I would like. I wonder," Dr. Greenwood looked briefly at Titus' closed door, "if you might be interested in a mutually beneficial business opportunity?"

Claire was confused. "I'm not sure what you mean."

"Hence the need for us to have a conversation outside the walls of this mausoleum. Would you be willing to join me for dinner at my hotel?"

She looked at him doubtfully.

"Strictly business, I assure you. We can even meet in the restaurant, if you'd like."

"Well, I suppose that would be all right. Where are you staying?"

"The Dorchester. Shall we say at eight?" He handed her a calling card.

Claire nodded. Even she knew that the Dorchester was one of the most expensive hotels in London. "You have a room at the Dorchester?"

"Certainly not, my dear girl. I have the entire top floor. See you there."

Stunned, she looked at the card. It read, "Dr. Aristotle Greenwood, Occult Detective," with "London, New York, Paris" in small letters at the bottom. Claire half expected it to burst into flame at any moment, but it did not. Slightly disappointed, she put it in her bag and went back to work cataloging a lot of uninspired Egyptian pottery.

~ ~ ~

Deep within the maze below the British Museum, a figure moved through the darkness, heading for its nest. Expertly, he moved through the stacks and aisles carrying a small bag behind him. After so many hours, days, weeks, months combing through the labyrinth, he had learned the layout better than probably any other creature knew it. Even the occasional rat had become used to seeing him shuffle through the darkness and no longer paid him any heed.

In his mind, he had charted so much that he could find his way anywhere, even in complete darkness. And yet, despite all of his efforts, his goal still eluded him. He had spent endless hours alone in abandoned offices, comparing layouts of the floors and all of the available catalogues without finding a clue to what he was seeking. Still, he had learned that so much of the British Museum was still uncatalogued and limited to lists of boxes received without any clue what had happened to them since.

But he knew it was here. It called to him, but not clearly enough that he could find it. Still, he felt it nearby. So every night, he went out among the boxes and cabinets and crates and shelves and displays looking for it. He knew in his mind exactly what he was seeking: three items that were part of a set. They should have been easy to find but the fact that he could not worried him. They were still here, he knew that, but someone might be hiding them on purpose. Perhaps someone had their own designs upon them, or even worse, wanted them for the same reason he did. That was why he had to hurry. Too much time had already elapsed and the window of opportunity was beginning to close.

And then there was the matter of the sacrifice.

Even if he could find the items that he needed, a living sacrifice was required. He had no issue with that. Human life, particularly the lives of others, meant nothing to him. It didn't even particularly matter what kind he used. Male, female, old, young, virgin. Any was fine. It was the blood that was the most important aspect. Still, he had already picked one out. It helped that his intended victim worked in the bowels of the museum and was frequently in the same areas he searched. Then a thought occurred to him. Perhaps she was the one who was hiding his prizes from him. Maybe she had found them long ago and meant to use them herself. He had meant to wait to take her until he found the items but, maybe, just maybe, he should take her first and find out what she knew. Even if she hadn't been hiding them, she might have seen them as part of her endless indexing and cataloging.

Finally burrowing through, he came to his nest. It was nothing more than a small space he had cleared in the midst of the thickest cabinets and shelves, but it was virtually impenetrable unless one knew where to wriggle through. It held the mattress from a small cot, some papers that had been well thumbed and read, a tiny lantern and a small idol.

It was the statue of an Egyptian man with the head of a jackal. In his right hand, the figure held a staff. In his left, an ankh. It was an idol in the shape of Anubis, the ancient Egyptian god of the dead. The depiction was based on the New Kingdom era, but he had always felt that there was an older, more powerful version during an even more ancient time. It had been that bit of speculation that had inspired his theories and sent him out into the desert. Soon, he would prove himself correct and reap the rewards of his beliefs.

He made himself comfortable on the floor and emptied the bag. There were a few scraps of food, mostly taken from the waste baskets of various offices or lunch bags that he had stolen. This time, however, he'd scored a bounty and took it out gingerly. It had been a long time since he had eaten something like this. He put the cake, with its 'Happy Birthday Ned' scribbled in red frosting, and placed it along with the rest of the food before Anubis. Then he bowed his head and chanted to it in the words of the Ancient Egyptians.

Alone in the basement of the British Museum, there was no one to hear him.

~ ~ ~

"You mean to say you've never dined here at the Dorchester before?" Dr. Greenwood asked Claire as he sipped on his glass of wine.

Feeling horribly under-dressed, Claire shook her head. "No, it's a bit out of my price range. It's quite lovely, though."

The Dorchester was one of the more modern hotels in London, and it had already established a reputation for being favored by high society and the rich. Claire wondered which one of those applied to her companion. The dining room was bustling with activity as some were arriving from an early night at the theater or about to enjoy a later evening in Piccadilly Circus. Everyone was dressed in their most elegant evening clothes, with some men in tuxedos and a few women in elegant evening gowns. Dr. Greenwood was dressed in the same white suit he had worn earlier to the museum. It was clear that he was a man who did as he liked and to hell with anyone who complained about it.

Claire, despite taking the time to run home and change into her best dress, felt poor in comparison to everyone else. She touched the string of fake pearls around her neck, certain that at any moment, they—and she—would be exposed as a fake. Clearly it was obvious to everyone that she did not belong here, that she was an imposter and a minute away from being hustled out the door.

Dr. Greenwood noticed her discomfort. Leaning forward, he said softly, "You needn't be worried, my dear. If you feel intimidated by these creatures, remember that each and every one of them also uses the toilet despite their embarrassment at such a base, normal function."

Claire stared at the man. If she had more of her wits about her, she'd have slapped him but, she had to admit, that realization did make things easier. There was something leveling about such a thought.

"Now, tell me about yourself," he said. "You said you come from New York, yes?"

"Brooklyn, actually. First in my family to graduate from college."

"Ah. Indeed, they must be quite proud of you?"

"I hope so. My mother is, but my father isn't entirely sure that I shouldn't be married with a mob of kids already."

Dr. Greenwood laughed. "Yes, my parents felt that I was an embarrassment with my unorthodox interests. It wasn't quite cricket, so to say."

"What are you interests, if I may ask?"

"Oh, they are many and varied. I am a seeker, you might say, looking for truth in the most unusual places. Indeed, I have traveled virtually across the globe in search of such artifacts. I keep them in my collection at my estate in Essex. You must come and see them some time."

The waiter brought their dinner, an excellently prepared pheasant with gravy and sautéed greens. Claire ate slowly and carefully, afraid of using the wrong utensil at the wrong time. Dr. Greenwood, however, dove into his dinner with a gusto that was rarely seen in polite company. He devoured it in a flurry, almost making it a point to use as many utensils in as haphazard an order as possible.

"I think I would like to see your collection," Claire responded. "Is it all ancient artifacts?"

"Oh, heavens no, there are just as many modern items that deserve consideration as well as ancient ones. The older ones may have more, shall we say, influence, but sometimes it is the impetuous of the new that make them so … well, effective, I suppose would be the right word. Yes, effective. There is often something about the modern that cuts directly to the point of things, don't you agree?"

Claire had no idea what he meant, but she agreed anyway.

"I hadn't thought of it that way, but I guess you may have a point. Something like how the Realist school of painting can be more definite than the Impressionists?"

"Quite so," Dr. Greenwood replied, rather thrilled that Claire had apparently understood what he had meant—even though she really hadn't.

The waiter cleared the dinner dishes promptly and returned minutes later with a dessert of chocolate mousse. It was, quite simply, the most delightful thing that Claire had ever tasted, and she said so.

Dr. Greenwood smiled. "Yes, the dessert chef is from Switzerland, I understand. It would be an insult to his national pride if he did not produce such wonders. But now, Miss Montgomery, down to, how you say, brass tacks? I need your help."

"Oh?" she said rather disappointed. "I thought perhaps you were going to offer me a job."

"Perhaps later, but right now you are of greater value to me in your current position."

"At the museum? How?"

Dr. Greenwood leaned in closer and lowered his voice. "What I have to tell you is very important. May I have your assurance that you will keep it, and your association with me, in confidence?"

Curious, Claire could not help but agree.

"Very well. I am looking for three certain items. They are a dagger, an amulet, and a headpiece. They were the property of a priest of Seth predating the first Egyptian dynasty. It is my belief that the tomb of this priest was found by Professor Abner Winslow several years ago. He went into the desert one day and he disappeared, along with his entire party. But, before that happened, he sent a crate back.

"I have spent years following that crate. It went through several hands, including an unscrupulous thief back in Cairo. From there it went to New York and then to Brazil, Paris, Amsterdam, and finally London. It is my belief that it was finally delivered, by mistake, to the very place it was supposed to go all along: the British Museum. It is there, somewhere, buried and forgotten. But it must be found, and soon!"

"Dr. Greenwood, I don't know what you're talking about. Didn't Titus already tell you we don't have it?"

"Titus is a blithering fool and you know it. He's nothing more than an annoying little man who, having gotten a taste of unexpected power, will do anything to keep it. For all I know, he's found the items already and is hiding them."

"Now, why would he do that? He's an archeologist, a professional."

"He's a professional buffoon is what he is. This isn't the first time I've come across him or the first time he's been a stumbling block to my investigations. Here, this is what I'm looking for. Have you seen them anywhere in the collection?"

He handed Claire a folded sheet of paper. A voice within her told her to refuse it, that this was a dangerous step that could get her in a lot of trouble. But the other part of her, the part that had driven her to pursue archaeology in the first place, wanted to see what they were. More than that, the intellectually curious part of her wanted to find them probably as much as Greenwood did.

She opened the paper and looked at the drawings. The headpiece was a simple skull cap with a few carvings along the rim. A notation next to it read "solid gold." The amulet was more decorative. It had an oval shaped gem in the center with an outside lining that looked as if lightning were issuing from the center. It rested on a simple chain.

The dagger, however, was ornate. The blade was not straight but in a sort of squiggle towards a tapered end. There was a more intricate drawing of the hilt which had strange hieroglyphics on it.

"It is the dagger of Seth," Dr. Greenwood said. "The legend is that it was crafted from a piece of a meteorite that landed in what became Egypt millions of years ago. It is an item of unbelievable power and must be destroyed. Have you seen it?"

Claire shook her head. None of the pieces looked at all familiar. But even if they had, she wouldn't have told him. Something in the way he said "destroyed" bothered her. Artifacts were meant to be studied and preserved. That he would even advocate such a thing meant that they were already on opposing sides.

"Are you sure you haven't seen them?"

She looked at the drawings again. They definitely weren't familiar. She knew, though, that they were not in the catalogue. But that, of course, didn't necessarily mean that they weren't in the museum.

"Why do you want to destroy them?"

Dr. Greenwood leaned back, sensing that he had already lost her confidence.

"I don't take such steps lightly, Miss Montgomery. When I do, I assure you that it is after careful deliberation and consideration. I am a protector of the past … and the future. I preserve where I can but that is not always possible."

"Your card said that you were an 'Occult Detective.' What does that mean?"

"It means what it says."

"What are you, a comic?"

"My apologies. For many years, I have dedicated myself to the investigation of the unknown. Where other scientists sneer and scoff, I explore. There are worlds, Miss Montgomery, other worlds that exist beside our own."

"You mean ghosts?"

He spread his hands in an open gesture. "Sometimes. But spirits are not the only things that dwell beyond. There are forces which were old when this world was young. They exist beyond the pale curtain of this realm, and they are forever seeking to find their way through to here."

Claire tried to think of any excuse she could make to escape as quickly as possible.

"I know your game, Dr. Greenwood. You see, when I was a little girl, my grandmother took me to Coney Island. Do you know why? To visit a psychic. This woman, who was a hundred years old if she was a day, saw my grandmother once a week, sometimes twice on Sunday, so she could 'channel' the spirit of my grandfather. So, without my mother knowing, she took me along one day to let me speak to my paw-paw. We get there and she goes into this whole spiel, moaning and groaning, eyes rolling up, and she starts talking in this weird voice. Of course, my grandmother thinks it's my paw-paw so she starts going on and on talking about the family and all. Then she gets to me, and the voice gets all excited. Claims I'm 'the one,' and I'm going to face lots of danger and have excitement and adventure. I'm going to be someone big and important. That's how I know she was full of it and so are you. What kind of adventure am I going to face stuck in the basement at the museum? I'm about as unimportant as a person can get. There are no such things as ghosts and this life is all there is, fella. End of story."

Dr. Greenwood stared at her and then, suddenly, began to laugh. It was a full laugh and the only real emotion she'd seen him show.

"Well, Miss Montgomery, in that case, I assume you're not interested in my offer." He started to get ready to leave.

"Whoa, hold on there, you never made an offer."

"Didn't I? How careless of me. If you have not seen these items, and I know that they're there, I need to search the museum holdings myself. I am prepared to offer you a handsome sum for such access."

Claire shook her head. "Access that Titus wouldn't give you, right?"

"Precisely."

She thought of all of the expenses she couldn't afford and the few luxuries that she hadn't allowed herself to wish for. But the risk was too great. Titus could have her blackballed and he would.

"No, I'm sorry. I can't. Titus would have a fit."

Dr. Greenwood stood up and grinned. "I understand perfectly, my dear. Please, let me give you my private telephone number here at the hotel. If you should see anything...unusual...please do give me a call. In the meantime, I will speak to your board of directors, even though it will waste more of my precious time."

"The board?" Claire suddenly became very nervous.

"Oh, rest assured that our little conversation will remain between us. I assume I can count on the same discretion from you as well?"

Her mouth suddenly dry, all she could do was nod.

"Splendid. Until we meet again, Miss Montgomery."

Dr. Greenwood shook her hand and headed for the exit. Claire noticed a large man, dressed in a black suit, detach himself from a position against the wall and follow him out. "What a strange pair," Claire thought, and stood up to leave when the waiter placed a bill in front of her.

"Oh, no, you don't understand. Dr. Greenwood was paying for dinner."

The waiter smiled as if he had experienced this many times when serving the doctor.

"The esteemed Doctor did indeed pay for his meal, Miss. He had me hold your check for you. I imagine he was unsure if he would cover it or not. As you can see, he did not. If you please?"

Claire stared at the bill. It was more than she made in a week. With her anger rising, she took her checkbook out of her bag and started writing.

~ ~ ~

He spent the night rummaging through the area next to where he had been a few nights before. He was certain that he was close. That crate bore every marking he was looking for but had only carried useless idols that he had sent back long ago. They were worthless items, really, but had been sent mostly to show the backers that he had been doing something. What he was looking for, what he needed, had to be close. He could feel them nearby.

Time was running out.

~ ~ ~

The next day, Claire made a point to be at work early.

Peabody did not have any other phantom events to report. He found nothing misplaced or thrown about during his morning shift. However, he had discovered one strange incident.

"Weirdest thing, Miss Claire, you know that paleontology lab down on the third sub-floor? Well, someone broke into their icebox down there. Cleared it out."

Claire thought it was odd that the paleontologists even had a fridge. "Were they keeping samples of something in there?"

"Nope. Just their food and lunches and such. I guess one of them is having a birthday today and there was a cake in there. Someone stole the whole kit and kaboodle."

"I guess being a phantom works up an appetite," Claire said jokingly, but Peabody didn't think it was very funny.

The bulk of her day was spent indexing various catalogued pieces into a formal list. It was back-breaking, mind-numbing work, something that made her regret ever having applied for her position. Titus had been in his office virtually most of the day, which was not surprising. Like a gopher, he stuck his head out of his hole only when he had to, and afraid it would get lopped off, vanished as quickly as possible.

Sometime in the afternoon, she heard his phone ring. Claire couldn't make out exactly what Titus was talking about, but he wasn't happy about something. "What? Now? Do you have any idea how much work I have?" he yelled loud enough to break through the barrier of the windows.

"Yes, yes, all right, fine. I'll be right up."

Moments later, Titus came out of his office and locked his door. "I've got to go upstairs. That damn Greenwood has gone and called a meeting of the board of directors. Apparently, they're fool enough to listen to him. Just keep on doing what you're doing, Montgomery. I probably won't be back before you leave. Make sure you finish those lists and that they're properly indexed, not like the last lot."

The last lot, Claire knew, had been mislabeled because he had gone in after and changed her notations only to find that she had been right all along. She accepted the lack of an apology, and even general civility, because she needed the position. And sadly, in a man's world, she'd come to expect the worst from men. She was generally not surprised to find her expectations, low as they were, even higher than reality.

She continued her work, and when the hour of her departure arrived, was prepared to leave for the day when she noticed a golden idol of Anubis on the floor outside Titus' door. It sat there, looking at her unapprovingly with its jackal gaze. She sighed to herself.

"Well, what are you doing out here?" she asked, not expecting an answer. Then she remembered that she had taken it out of Titus' office the other day to examine it for the index. Because the office had been locked afterwards, she could not put it back.

"So what am I going to do with you?" She couldn't leave it out there. Whether she believed it or not, Peabody's phantom might snatch it, and in any case, a solid gold idol would be too much of a temptation. She'd have to put it back.

Claire bent down and peered inside the lock. It did not look particularly sophisticated. She'd seen a lot sturdier during her childhood in Brooklyn, and few could match her lock-picking skills back then. She took a pin out of her hair, straightened it, and began to fiddle with the lock. It gave way with an ease that was almost embarrassing. She opened the door and saw the spot she had taken it from before, on a shelf near the top of the back wall.

Surprised again at the weight of such a small thing, Claire picked it up and carefully put it back up where it belonged. A layer of dust cascaded down and made her sneeze. When she did, she noticed a box she hadn't seen before hidden in the corner of the office. It was a wooden crate, much like the one the phantom had allegedly rifled through the other day. Curious, she walked over to it. There were some books and papers placed purposefully on top, as though to hide it and make it appear ordinary and nondescript. She removed them and saw, in plain block letters printed on the crate, "From Abner Winslow, Cairo, Egypt" and addressed to "British Museum, London, England." Her hands were shaking as she pulled the crate out into the light and opened the lid.

There, sitting quietly, were the three items that Dr. Greenwood had described to her just the previous evening. The skullcap. The amulet. The dagger of Seth. They had obviously been hidden there for some purpose. All three items shone in the weak light, and Claire felt herself breathing sharply as she looked at them. They were quite possibly the most beautiful Egyptian relics she'd ever seen. She lightly brushed her fingers across them, feeling the engravings. It was clear that Titus had been lying to Greenwood. He'd had these all along.

She picked up the phone and dialed for the operator, who connected her to the Dorchester and the top floor. The phone rang for what seemed like a horribly long time when Dr. Greenwood's voice finally came on the line.

"Yes," he said.

"Dr. Greenwood, its Claire Montgomery at the museum. You were right. They are here. Titus has had them in his office all this time. Even when he was speaking to you!"

She could feel the anger coming through the phone.

"That bastard!" he yelled. "What does he think he's playing at? He told the board that he'd never heard of them, never seen them. I just got back from the meeting. Where are you right now?"

Claire held the phone close to her face. "I'm in his office. I'm going to take these out in my bag. Can you meet me?"

Dr. Greenwood replied, but all Claire could hear was the sound of Titus' voice behind her.

"What are you doing in my office?" He was yelling and almost on the verge of a spasm from anger.

She did not put the phone down.

"Dr. Titus," she said as she tried to sound as calm as possible. "I didn't hear you come in. I was just putting the idol of Anubis back. I... I didn't want to leave it out unlocked."

Titus moved forward.

"Who are you talking to?"

"Oh," she was becoming more nervous but was trying to hide it and was failing. "It's just my young man. I'm telling him to meet me at the Lyceum tonight. We're...we're going to a play."

Titus spied the crate, moved out into the light and the open space.

"I'm afraid that you're going to miss the theatre tonight, Miss Montgomery. I need you to...work late."

He drew back and hit her square in the face. Claire fell back and hit her head upon the open crate. She was unconscious immediately.

"Miss Montgomery? Miss Montgomery!" Dr. Greenwood's voice rang from the phone.

Titus picked up the receiver. "Isn't she rather young for you, Aristotle?" he said, and hung up the phone.

Hidden in the stacks, a dark figure had seen everything. Moving silently, it came closer, and just as Titus sensed its presence, the figure struck the curator on the head, knocking him out. Now it had to make a choice. There was an unexpected wealth of opportunities. It had planned to use the girl for the ceremony but there was a bit of joyful irony in replacing her with Titus. It put the items in a bag and, swiftly, dragged Titus along and walked away.

~ ~ ~

75

As she was coming to, Claire could see two blurred figures in her immediate field of vision, both of them staring down at her.

"Miss Montgomery," said a voice near her. "You need to wake up. We're running out of time."

As she blinked, the fog fell away from her eyes and she recognized the figures as Dr. Greenwood and his large companion. She tried to sit up and was rewarded with a lightning blast of pain in her head.

"You have to move slowly, my dear," Dr. Greenwood said. "You've taken a nasty knock on your head. Do you recognize me? Do you know where you are?"

"Yeah," Claire said, "you're the guy yelling in my face. What happened?"

Dr. Greenwood straightened up and helped Claire to Titus' desk chair.

"You called me from here saying that Titus had the artifacts then I heard him hit you. Matthew and I came as quickly as possible."

"Right, I remember that. He caught me in here, looking at the artifacts. I guess my bluff didn't work so well after all."

She looked over at the empty crate and sighed.

"I guess he took it on the lam. Sorry, Doctor."

From the front of the office, Matthew spoke.

"No. He was taken. Look here." He pointed at a blood stain on the floor.

"You mean someone jumped him after he conked me on the head?"

The large man nodded. "There are signs here. A quick struggle, then a body dragged out of here."

"How long ago?" asked the doctor.

"Twenty minutes at most."

"Can you track him?"

Matthew stared down at the floor.

"Very difficult, but yes."

Dr. Greenwood reached into his coat pocket and took out what looked like some sort of iron lodestone. The object pulsated with a sickly red glow, almost like a heartbeat.

"Quickly, Matthew. And you too, Miss Montgomery. We don't have a minute to spare."

Without a word, Matthew bounded out of the door and down the corridor. Dr. Greenwood grabbed Claire by the wrist and pulled her along before she could say a word.

~ ~ ~

"Do you like it? I made it especially for you. Well, not really. I was going to use your assistant but this is so much better, don't you think?"

Titus tried to sit up but couldn't. His wrists and ankles were chained. He was lying on a table of some sort. It wasn't stone, but it didn't feel like wood either. He could hear the voice but couldn't see who was speaking. The only thing he could see was that he was in a large space, about the size of a garage, and there were mummies positioned around him in a circle. He could only see three of them, but he assumed there was another behind his head. He struggled but could not break free. His mouth was gagged, and every time he tried to speak, he ended up choking.

The voice continued to speak behind him. It sounded odd and cracked, as if it's owner had not spoken in some time.

"You never thought my work was worth anything. You belittled me every chance you had, buried my research and now, when you realize only a sliver of their importance, you tried to steal them from me. But no longer, Titus. Now you shall help me prove my greatest theory."

The speaker moved in front of Titus and he could finally see what had been stalking the catacombs beneath the British Museum. Abner Winslow stood in full Egyptian priest dress, but on his head was the gold skull cap and around his neck hung the amulet. He cradled the dagger of Seth fondly. The man's hair and beard were dirty and mottled with dust and cobwebs, and his eyes were the picture of madness.

Slowly, Winslow began chanting, but in a language older than ancient Egyptian. It was a language that was old when the world was young and creatures roamed the earth that no sane man had ever known. Titus struggled against the chains but it was no use. He wasn't going anywhere.

~ ~ ~

They could hear the chanting coming from somewhere ahead of them, but they couldn't figure out where.

The area was cluttered with shelving units that went nearly up to the ceiling, disappearing into the darkness. Every aisle they went down came to a dead end. They were stuck in a maze that, for all tey knew, had no solution. The chanting grew louder and louder, and Claire thought she could hear the sound of someone's muffled yells.

"It's got to be close," she said, "but what the heck is he doing?"

"Playing a very dangerous game," answered Dr. Greenwood, "and one that might kill us all."

Matthew was studying the floor. There were scratch marks there that could barely be seen in the darkness. His eye followed them to a thick cabinet off to one side of the stacks. He went over, grabbed its corner and pulled. It moved slowly but it opened. Ducking low, they all crawled under the shelves piled high above them only to find themselves in another aisle. They ran down it quickly, Matthew in the lead, Claire in the middle and Dr. Greenwood wheezing behind them. Claire didn't know why, but she felt the need to hurry—and the nagging fear that they might already be too late.

~ ~ ~

Slowly, the mummies started to move. At first it was just a twitch or two, but they eventually started walking toward Titus. Winslow had been expecting this. He'd even been able to accomplish it a few times before, but it was useless without the dagger and the sacrifice. Titus' eyes were wide open, unable to believe what he was seeing. The mummies came and knelt around him, waiting.

Winslow continued to chant, feeling the words carry him forward. He moved and swayed and, as the ritual reached its climax, he plunged the dagger of Seth straight into Titus' heart.

Titus screamed briefly and then he was gone. Out of the wound streamed blood and something else. A vague vapor trail oozed out, lingered briefly above his body and then dived directly into each of the mummies. They were thrown back from the force of the invasion.

As they got slowly to their feet, they began to change. The wrappings fell away from them onto the floor. Their bodies morphed and changed, bathed in an eerie glow. Where before had been mummies, ancient corpses, now stood four Egyptian gods: Anubis, the protector of the dead, with his jackal head; Bastet, the goddess of pleasure, purring from her cat's head; Thoth, god of knowledge and the head of an ibis; and, lastly, Osiris, king of the gods, who had been killed and resurrected. They walked towards Winslow who had supplicated himself before them.

"Mortal, you have called and we have answered. What is your wish?"

Winslow looked up and smiled.

~ ~ ~

"Oh, hell," Claire whispered. "This isn't good."

They had gotten to the hidden area just in time to see Winslow sacrifice Titus. Matthew had pushed them aside and out of view, and signaled with his hands for them to stay there while he tried to circle around.

"You got anything to handle this, Doctor?" Claire asked, not expecting a response.

"I just might," he replied and held up a golden ankh, the symbol of life in ancient Egypt.

"What are you going to do with that?" Claire asked. "Hit him over the head with it?"

"Hardly," he responded. "We must wait for Matthew's signal."

~ ~ ~

79

Winslow looked at the gods with an expression of pure joy. He had called them and they had come. Now, he would ask his boon.

"Oh, mighty Osiris, I ask for only one thing. I am a seeker of truth. I desire knowledge above all things. I ask you to give me the names of those who came before you—before Nut, Shu and Geb. Tell me of the Old Ones."

Osiris looked at the man before him and took his measure. Finally, as he was about to speak, another voice filled the chamber.

"It is not for Osiris to speak of these things, nor for you to hear, mortal fool. They have always been here."

A wind began to blow from out of nowhere, swirling around the space. It moved at a terrific pace and began to even make the gods step back. In the center was Winslow... and something else.

From the center of the cyclone, a vast form was rising, breaking through the cement floor. It grew larger and larger until it dwarfed everything else. It had the shape of a man but the head of a pig and it grunted hideously as it rose from its stygian depths.

"You are not worthy of this knowledge," said the fearsome being. "Your impudence shames you and exposes you to my darkness. I am Setekh, maker of the weapon you dishonor, and I bring to you the Mark of Chaos."

With a gesture, Setekh unleashed a golden coil that wrapped itself around Winslow. Within seconds, the coil tightened mercilessly, until Winslow was literally ripped apart.

Unable to control herself, Claire screamed.

"Did you think I would allow you to return to life yet again, Osiris?" Setekh grunted. "I am, and always will be, the bringer of your death!"

Setekh set his coil upon Osiris, who resisted but was driven to his knees.

"Yes!" Setekh screeched. "Kneel before me, as you should have done thousands of years ago."

A loud whistle filled the space, and Matthew threw himself at Setekh. The enormous man-beast battered the man aside with ease. The other gods moved back in terror, unable to protect themselves from the walking chaos before them.

Before Claire could stop him, Dr. Greenwood leaped forward and brandished the ankh at the giant god. Satekh looked at the object and laughed. He threw Dr. Greenwood back against the wall and turned his attention back to Osiris, who was succumbing to the pressure of the golden coil.

Carefully, Claire crept out of her hiding space and over to Dr. Greenwood. He handed her the ankh and motioned for her to point it at Setekh.

"You tried that already! What good will it do? We need to get out of here!"

"No, I was foolish. This is the Ankh of Isis. You have to wield it, not me."

Something clicked in her mind and she understood. Of course. She had to be the one to use the ankh. Isis was the wife of Osiris. It was she who had resurrected her husband after he had been killed by Setekh. No man could use her symbol and make it work.

Claire took the ankh and held it up high, pointing it at Setekh's huge, porcine face.

"Hey, ugly!" she yelled. "Look over here! I've got something for you!"

Setekh turned, and this time, terror spread over his face.

Rays of sunlight emanated from the ankh, striking Setekh in the chest. The giant god stumbled but did not fall. He struggled back and started to come forward towards Claire. Not even aware she was doing it, she began uttering a prayer to Isis.

In the midst of the blinding light, another figure formed. It was a woman. Tall, majestic, and powerful. Isis, the Egyptian "mother of god," had come.

"You have no power here," she said to Setekh.

The god of chaos faced her and let loose his cord, but Isis caught it easily and melted it away. Setekh directed his full force against her, but she walked through it and placed her hands on either side of his head. Softly, powerfully, Isis compressed Setekh, pushing him down and back into the ground. As the mother god forced him back to the blackness of chaos, Setekh tried desperately to push back at her, push her away. Finding no purchase, he fell ever downward.

In a final blaze of light and force, Isis drove Setekh back into the earth until they both disappeared in a sudden explosion that blinded Claire and Dr. Greenwood. When their eyes adjusted, they found themselves alone in the empty space. The bodies of Titus and Winslow were gone, and all that remained were lifeless mummies, returned to their normal state. Matthew, unconscious on the other side of the room, had seen nothing. The relics lay on the floor, looking deceptively harmless.

~ ~ ~

"I was saddened to hear of your termination," Dr. Greenwood said as they ate their lunch at the Savoy.

"Yeah," Claire said. "Me too. When Titus 'disappeared,' the board brought in a new director for the Egyptology Department. And the new department head, of course, brought his own people with him. Now I'm out of a job. But you've never really explained to me what happened down there that night."

"What's to explain? You saw it all with your own eyes."

"Sure, but who was that guy who killed Titus?"

"Ah," said Dr. Greenwood, taking a sip of his cocktail, "that was the unfortunate Professor Winslow, late of Egypt."

"But wasn't he the one who found the relics in the first place?"

"Indeed. But at the time, he was ignorant of their purpose or power. Once he'd discovered certain scrolls in a forgotten tomb in the desert, he realized what he had let slip through his fingers and he had to find them again."

Not sure of who'd be paying for the lunch, Claire had made certain to order only a light salad and a glass of water. Her bank account still hadn't recovered from their dinner at the Dorchester.

"So he sneaked back here to London where he spent nearly a year living in the lower levels of the museum, searching for his crate," Dr. Greenwood explained. "There was no way he could know that his crate didn't arrive here until recently, so he was searching for something that wasn't even here."

"Why didn't the crate get here earlier?" Claire asked.

"Well, that was due to the malfeasance of a certain miscreant named Sarenpet back in Cairo. Someone had stolen the crate out of the shipping office and sold it to Sarenpet, who had sent it on a smuggling trip through several major cities until, quite by accident, it was discovered by the police and sent on its way to the original destination. Our late friend Titus recognized the pieces and had some idea of what they were worth and what they meant. I'm unsure if he planned to resell the relics or use them himself in the ritual."

Claire shook her head. "I still can't get that whole scene out of my head. What was that ritual meant to accomplish?"

"It reanimated the Egyptian gods so the caster could ask a boon of them. They are bound by the ritual to answer any question put to them, no matter what it is."

"And that's what Winslow asked for?"

"Indeed. It has always been one of his theories that this world was once the realm of older creatures, and that one of them created mankind as an 'accident.' I confess that this is not a new theory to me. Perhaps if he had consulted me, I might have been able to persuade him to abandon this path."

"Well, I guess it all makes some kind of sense, but I'm still out of a job."

Dr. Greenwood wiped his mouth with his napkin. "I might be able to be of some assistance in that regard. It turns out that I have need of a cataloguer at my estate, and you have proven yourself to be very resourceful. I'd be happy to offer you the position."

Claire looked at him warily, wondering if she should hitch her cart to this guy. In the end, she had no choice. It wasn't as if any other museum was knocking at her door.

"Okay, I accept," she said. "But not as a cataloguer or indexer. Considering that you wouldn't have even gotten out of this mess without me, and considering that you owe me for starting this whole thing that got me fired, and considering that dinner at the Dorchester, I'm not your employee. I'm either your partner, or there's no goddamn deal!"

Dr. Greenwood smiled, but there was a hint of chiding in his response. "Really, Miss Montgomery," he said, "this is hardly the place for profanity!"

WHISPERS FROM THE DREAD WORLD

by Duane Spurlock

UNO

Tenochtitlán, 1380

He was a warrior. For the city-state of Tlaxcala. A mighty warrior. Many men had fallen beneath his swinging weapons.

But now his arms were bound behind him. He was one of many dressed in brilliantly ornamented costumes, fellow warriors from Tlaxcala, slowly advancing in single file toward a scarlet-spattered slaughter stone. Their fate was determined during the *xochiyaóyotl*—the ritual Flower War between city states—when the greater numbers from Tenochtitlán swarmed over their group.

Like his comrades in arms, he was destined to die a glorious death. His blood would be slung into the air and would soak into the earth. It would appease the gods and bring good fortune to his people. For this reason, the lesser priests—one on each side of him—demonstrated their great respect as they guided him to the altar. At each gentle pressure on his shoulders from the hands of the priests, he would take another step forward. It was so for all the captive warriors making their way to the altar, each accompanied by a pair of priests. Quiet. Dignified.

The warrior from Tlaxcala cared nothing for their respect. He didn't particularly care about the honor he would be doing his gods or his people. Partly, he knew, his detachment came from the beverage he was given in an ornate goblet before the slow march began to the slaughter stone. The drink was meant to calm excitable candidates and enhance one's perceptions of the spirit world—the next world, the one into which he would step as he passed under the arch of his own blood as it spewed skyward.

And so he ceased watching the progression toward glory before him and gazed at the remarkable skies—so bright. The edges of the monumental structures seemed incised against the air. The outlines of the wheeling birds appeared knife sharp. Perhaps they were representatives of the gods—or the gods themselves, come to witness their human slaves' obeisance to their tremendous powers.

The warrior ignored the colorfully dressed crowds swarming in the plaza below. A roaring filled his ears, so he did not hear their chants, their cries to the terrible gods they served. Nor did he notice the shouts from a hundred throats that interrupted the other noises: "Blood! Blood! Blood!"

The platform on which he and the other captives stood with the priests was far from the largest in Tenochtitlán. Despite the crowd of worshippers, this ceremony was subsidiary to those of the major temple and the great priest. The Great Pyramid rose still higher than this platform.

Here, his escort to the gods was but a minor priest, although he had attracted a great body of worshippers. Even in Tlaxcala the warrior had heard of this priest, for he was known as a sort of showman. He was called The Jaguar.

Perhaps the warrior from Tlaxcala should have felt honored to be dispatched to the gods by such a famed figure. But the drink in the goblet had lessened his cares for this world.

He watched now as the priest tossed a streaming heart onto a chacmool—a stone figure that reclined near the altar, its face turned to the side, a platter balanced on its stomach. On this salver rested a steaming pile of fist-sized hearts.

It was now the turn of the captive before the warrior to approach the slaughter stone. The warrior watched as The Jaguar raised his hand. He intoned words the man from Tlaxcala could not hear, then drove his fist to the chest of the sacrifice. The warrior was roused from his stupor when he saw—he could swear he saw—The Jaguar's blood-covered face and head change, to vibrate into some other shape for a snap of a moment. A thrill raced through the warrior's limbs, and he wondered if this vision was caused by the spirit drink he had swallowed.

The Jaguar raised the still-pumping heart. Blood poured down his red-bathed arms as he pushed away the twitching body, which the lesser priests began to dismember before flinging its limbs to the four corners of the horizon.

The Jaguar tossed the heart to the pile on the chacmool, then gestured.

The warrior's escorts led him to his place. He felt the slaughter stone against the backs of his legs. He faced The Jaguar. The priest's features and his raiment—plumed robe, painted bones, gold bangles and chains—were drenched in blood. Crimson dripped from his nose and chin, ran from his brows. The Jaguar grinned and his stained teeth glowed within his scarlet face.

The priest extended his arm overhead. The warrior saw, then, The Jaguar held no knife. The arm dropped, the flattened hand drove into the warrior's chest with no more resistance than if he'd pushed his fist into a bowl of corn meal mush. Lightning flashed behind the warrior's eyes. Blinded for a moment, he realized, I am no longer a warrior. I am a sacrifice.

He saw the priest's eyes turn green. The Jaguar's face moved and changed, his jaws opened to reveal long, cat-like fangs. He held the warrior's heart in his fist.

All colors in the warrior's sight turned to red. His knees began to buckle. He felt the hands of the lesser priests grab his arms. They supported him as The Jaguar bit into the streaming blood muscle.

The red shifted to purple. And the purple deepened to black. And the warrior felt nothing more.

DOS
Mexico City, 1974

In the basement of Museo Nacional de Antropología, Jorge Vazquez unlocked the steel door to the prep room. Here he would be overseeing the installation of the museum's newest exhibit—to Jorge's mind, a very remarkable one.

An archaeological team from one of the local universities discovered a mummy near the large temple complex—Templo Mayor—of the Aztec capital, Tenochtitlán, upon whose ruins Mexico City now stood. Not so many Aztec mummies had ever been found, because the Aztecs cremated most rulers and other important people, so the find was remarkable for its rarity alone.

But Jorge considered the mummy even more significant because of its bindings. Never had he heard of a mummy like this one!

It was shrouded in leather. And it was strapped by wide bands of leather to a large slab of stone, whose entire surface was carved over with Aztec pictographic writing. One of Jorge's colleagues, Gabriel Lopez, had started working on a translation as soon as the mummy, wrapped on its slab, arrived at the museum.

No one could yet explain why the leather had not deteriorated over the centuries it spent underground. Perhaps, one of the archaeologists had surmised, a method of tanning leather—some technique lost to the modern world—was behind the inexplicable preservation of the shroud and straps.

Stepping into the preparation room, Jorge was surprised to find the lights shut off. And he was disappointed that his assistant, Oscar, was not here to greet him. Plenty of workers should have been filling the room with activity. What did this mean?

Jorge switched on the overhead fluorescents, which blinked into life. Tables and cabinets were set up, ready for work to start. "Oscar!" Jorge called. "Oscar! Where are you?" Where, for that matter, was the security guard, Ricardo? He normally met Jorge on the other side of the steel door. Was this some sort of prank? If so, Jorge was not pleased.

He hoped nothing had happened to the mummy. Jorge had already been dismayed when the package arrived with some damage sustained during transport from the dig site. The slab of carved stone carrying the mummy through eternity had been cracked near one corner.

"Oscar!" Jorge's voice rang with a metallic echo in the large room.

He stepped around two reclining figures carved from stone—chacmools—and recalled that one from the exhibit halls was due for touching up, but didn't know two were going to be cluttering the prep room while the important work on his new mummy was going on. Jorge walked to the rear of the room. He examined the objects on the prep tables, where everything was arranged for work.

The slab had been placed on a large wooden pallet positioned in the rear corner of the room near the overhead door—now closed—to a vast storage room and by the wall opposite the double doors of the freight elevator. The elevator shaft led to the loading dock and the museum's exhibit floors above.

Jorge stopped moving when he reached the slab. He stared.

The slab remained on the pallet. But the leather straps and shroud were piled loosely on the floor.

Where was the body that was supposed to be wrapped in the shroud?

Was this some terrible joke?

Jorge could barely breathe. His throat felt constricted. His face was hot. He trembled as he fought with competing urges to scream or run to the telephone.

Finally he turned to make a call. The phone sat on one of the tables near the entrance. After he took two steps, the fluorescents flickered and blinked out. Paralyzed by surprise, Jorge didn't move. Then he saw something—even in the complete darkness of this underground room, he saw something. Two feet from where he stood.

Two glowing green eyes.

He felt a sudden, crushing weight on his chest. He heard and felt bones snapping. Jorge tried to scream, but no sounds came from his open mouth—he seemed to have a large stone lodged in his throat.

Red rimmed his sight. The last things he saw were the green eyes floating in the dark.

TRES
The Dread World

El Puño de Bronce awoke. He was in a cave or some other dimly lit enclosed space.

He awoke in the middle of a fight.

He didn't remember falling asleep, but this sort of thing wasn't unusual in Hell.

El Puño wasn't sure if this place really was a part of Hell. The inhabitants called it the Dread World. If it wasn't part of Hell, it should have been.

The wrestler twisted in the grip of many hands. They held his arms, clutched at his torn clothes, pulled at the edge of his mask, squeezed his throat. Fists beat his chest, his face, his ribs.

The thing El Puño fought had eyes that seemed to glow green. Its face was human and painted black, red and yellow in ceremonial Aztec designs for battle. It had more than a dozen arms; no body—the shoulders of the arms all melded in a knot where the chest and abdomen should have been. It stood on two arms, using hands instead of feet on the stone floor.

El Puño's back pressed against a rough sturdy surface like a wall. The luchador managed to raise one knee and wedged it between his body and the many-armed beast. He kicked out, and some of the hands lost their grips. He kicked again, and the creature flailed backwards. It never completely fell to the floor because any of its hands could act as feet, so it landed on two or three or four of its hands and remained upright.

El Puño rushed in and grabbed two wrists. He swung the thing off the floor and around. It slammed into the wall that had been supporting the luchador. El Puño rushed it again before it scrambled upright. He pummeled the painted face.

The thing didn't cry out. It made a slight grimace, then its many hands clutched his arms. It squeezed his head between two hands. Four hands were on the floor, and the thing began to push the luchador's mighty bulk backwards.

"El Puño de Bronce—I know of you," the thing said. "All of us here have heard of you."

"You speak Spanish—very well," El Puño managed to pant.

"You have been here enough to know that's how it is here."

El Puño grunted.

"You are a mighty warrior—I see that," the thing said, still pushing against the luchador, moving him back step by step. "I was a mighty warrior once. I still can recognize mightiness in another."

"Who—are you?"

"I was from Tlaxcala. But I don't remember my name. I lost that when I came here." He continued to press against his opponent's resistance. "You still have your name. Leave before you lose it. And more."

"You know me," El Puño grunted. "You know why I am here?"

"Yes. But you search in vain." And then, as if El Puño weighed no more than a wad of paper, the thing flung the luchador upward.

QUATTRO
The Waking World

Scrubby bushes dotted the plain. A lizard curled around the shadow of a stone. The wind, low but steady, carried occasional pieces of grit from some faraway slope.

The lizard scampered away as the earth puckered—just like the mouth of a wrinkled old man getting ready to spit. But this mouth was four feet wide.

Then the pucker blew out a figure with a tremendous and dusty *spew!* A dirty cloud billowed up for a moment, then the mouth flattened out and disappeared.

The figure blown into the air was El Puño de Bronce. He pinwheeled twenty feet upward before tumbling to the ground. His impact threw a brown cloud into the wind, which carried it away.

He landed on his side, three feet from the battered edge of a paved highway.

When he opened his eyes three hours later, a young man was bent over and looking down at him. He was in his early twenties. A sparse mustache shadowed his upper lip. "Hey, *hombre*," he said. "Are you alive?"

El Puño blinked. "So far. *Sí*."

The young man said, "*Soy Raoul*," and he extended a hand. The luchador grasped it, and Raoul helped pull the masked man to his feet. El Puño groaned.

Raoul shook his head. "Whoof, you're a big one."

El Puño was an inch short of six feet and broadly muscled. What remained of his clothing was dusty and tattered. His mask was filthy and torn. One shoe was missing. His lips were cracked and swollen and his eyes were blackened.

The young man gestured at a dented Ford pickup stopped on the highway. "*A dónde vas?*"

"Wherever you're going." El Puño walked to the truck. He rested his hand on the passenger door handle, then said, "I'm going to stretch out in the back."

His rescuer made a face that didn't hide his belief that the big man was crazy. Then he got behind the wheel. Both the vehicle and El Puño made noises as the fighter climbed into the truck bed. The engine sputtered and then roared into life, Raoul let out the clutch, and the pickup rattled down the road. The jarring ride didn't stop El Puño from passing out into sleep.

CINCO

Jaime Guerrero had worked at the Museo Nacional de Antropología nearly a decade, almost since it had opened its doors. In all that time, never had he sensed such anxiety among the staff as he had in the last week.

Jaime was part of the maintenance crew. His days were filled with odd jobs—from changing light bulbs to necessary janitorial duties, to repairing and painting walls or exhibit fixtures. As a result, he knew everyone who worked at the museum from the lowest rung to the top of the ladder, plus many of the frequent visitors.

So he knew very well the men about whom the staff was whispering: Jorge Vazquez, his assistant Oscar Peña and Ricardo Ramirez had not been seen for four days. It was very unusual. Everyone was aware of Profesor Vazquez's excitement about the new mummy, Oscar was remarkably dutiful to El Profesor's enthusiasms, and Ricardo was reliable to a fault. Jaime couldn't recall a single day Ricardo had called into work sick during the five years since he'd joined the security department.

The museum's director normally displayed a brusque manner. When he began barking at the staff over the last two days, their anxiety increased. Jaime was surprised earlier today when the director asked in his usual gruff manner for the maintenance man to stay late. When Jaime arrived at the director's office after everyone but the remaining two security guards had left for the evening, his boss introduced him to a stranger.

"This is Juan Montez. He is looking into Profesor Vazquez's disappearance. Show him around the museum, wherever he wants to go." To Montez, the director said, "Jaime is the most trustworthy employee for El Museo Nacional de Antropología. It is his home, in many ways."

Jaime was surprised and humbled by El Director's words. Leaving the administrative office, Jaime led the investigator toward the galleries. Juan Montez was dressed a little too casually for Jaime's taste. "You are a detective?" he asked.

"Private."

"Ah. Like on TV."

"Not so glamorous and exciting. I dodge bill collectors more than bullets."

"Why not the police?"

Montez shrugged. "Your *jefe* doesn't want to stir up any scandal about the museum. Particularly after the big news about the new mummy."

"Hasn't anyone else reported El Profesor missing?"

"He has no family," Montez answered. "No wife, kids…nada."

"But he teaches."

"When this mummy was found, he asked the university for a sabbatical in the middle of the term to work on getting it displayed. It's some kind of big deal." Montez shrugged. "No one is missing him."

"Oscar? Ricardo?"

"Families, *si*. But your boss told them to say nothing to anyone. He's gonna take care of it. Again, no scandal in the news."

"Hm."

Jaime showed Montez through the public rooms. He had picked up enough information through the years by reading the exhibit signs and listening to the docents that he could answer all the detective's questions. He showed the investigator the office Vazquez used—small, not much more than a large closet, but tidy, its papers and books ordered and straight. Then Montez asked, "What about this *momia?*"

Jaime led him to the basement prep room. The tools and camera were still arrayed on the tables, and the mummy's slab, leather bands and shroud still rested at the back of the room. Two massive stone carvings sat near the door. As they passed the pair, Montez asked, "What's that?"

"Chacmools. Used for human sacrifices by the Aztecs. Usually in Gallery Four, but down here for some cleaning." Jaime shook his head. "El Profesor says they may have killed a hundred people a day."

"Mexico's not so different now, eh? The streets run with blood. But now it's the gangsters and bad politicians to watch out for."

Montez walked to the end of the room. Jaime joined him. "So the mummy's gone," the detective said, "but all its gear is still here."

Jaime nodded. "Why would someone do that?"

"You tell me. El Director is pulling his hair out thinking Vazquez took it, but he also can't believe he would do that."

"Steal the mummy?" Jaime nearly staggered with surprise. "El Profesor would never do that! Why?"

Montez stood over the slab and tried to make sense of its carvings. "Maybe to sell to a collector? Worth a lot of money, y'know? Maybe this Oscar and Ricardo helped him for a split of the cash."

Jaime sputtered. "I can't believe it!"

The fluorescents flickered. Both men turned toward the door. No one was there. But something in the air felt different. Both men felt a change in the room.

A cold tingle swept across the back of Jaime's neck. Then a low growl made the two men whirl about.

They faced a freakish figure. It was thin, hunched over, but still its height matched theirs. It was naked and its skin was a dull black stretched over its bones. Its limbs and the features of its face were twisted like a wrinkled dish rag that had been tightly wrung to squeeze out every drop of water. It didn't appear to breathe. It simply stood there. For all those strange details, the thing was recognizable as a man—or having been a man.

Jaime's heart hammered in his chest. Neither he nor Montez seemed able to move.

The detective spoke: "Where'd that come from?"

"*No lo sé.*"

"What is it?"

Jaime shook his head. Then the thing opened its eyes.

The eyes were green and glowed even against the brightness of the fluorescents. Jaime felt the skin tighten between his shoulder blades, and he knew he could no longer will himself to move from this spot.

The thing slowly raised both arms. The twisted flesh was lashed about the long bones of both limbs in impossible ways. It extended its hands toward the men. Its fingers were curled into tight knots that hardly looked like fists.

Jaime heard a thick purring. He realized after a few moments the sound came from the black thing.

Using its bent legs, it took a weaving step forward.

Jaime heard something new: Montez whimpering.

SEIS

Gabriel Lopez had spent hours at his kitchen table hunched over the photographs and rubbings taken from the slab on which the new mummy had been found. Since Jorge Vazquez had summoned him to translate the stone's carvings, Gabriel had eaten only one meal a day and slept two hours a night. Jorge's excitement about the find was infectious. It was that way with Jorge, and Gabriel was always swept along—so Gabriel's wife said before she left, taking their daughter with her. She was right, of course. Gabriel was bald now, his mustache and goatee were a scholarly gray, and his shoulders were permanently rounded from years of pouring over documents. Yet whenever Jorge called, Gabriel felt the thrill of a young man's excitement and enthusiasm for his work.

Gabriel had come to El Museo Nacional de Antropología to view the mummy's slab in person once again. He'd encountered the Museum's director at the front door as the man was leaving for the night. Only then did Gabriel learn that Jorge and the mummy were missing.

As he made his way to the preparation room, Gabriel's mind struggled against the surprise and confusion El Director's news had caused. His attention was consumed with this fresh mystery as he opened the door and entered the prep room.

He stopped just inside the door. Someone was here already. Gabriel started to speak, but his words went unspoken.

A thin figure stood near the rear of the room, hunched over, its back to him. It was naked, and its dull black flesh was wrapped strangely about its limbs. Two crumpled bodies, spattered with red, lay at its feet.

Gabriel couldn't speak. He couldn't move.

The figure straightened. It was nearly six feet tall. It turned slowly toward Gabriel. He saw its twisted, shrunken face. Gabriel was reminded of bodies he'd seen pulled from Irish bogs—compressed by the weight of the preserving soil for hundreds of years.

The thing's eyes were closed, giving its head the look of a blackened skull. Blood dripped from its chin. Then, weirdly, its features began to shift—its face grew fuller, but the marks of the creases remained. As Gabriel watched, the flesh of the thing's body grew less gaunt and the lines of its bones became less evident—like an inflated balloon that had, over time, lost its air until it shrank to a curdled piece of rubber, and now was being filled again. Years ago, Gabriel had made many treks to archaeological sites on horseback. The sound he heard from the thing's skin was like the creaking of saddle leather.

The figure raised a gnarled fist. The fingers unknotted and their twig-like appearance changed, grew stronger. The nail of each finger was shiny, like obsidian.

Gabriel's breath rasped in his throat. His feet shifted. The thing before him gestured, and he heard the door behind him slam shut.

Gabriel blinked, and the creature was suddenly before him—tall, and somehow imperious despite its nakedness. Its eyes opened, and their green glow pushed away every other color in the room. Gabriel watched as the thing's hand slowly sliced into his chest. He felt his bones snap—the sounds like gunshots in his ears—and the grating of his ribs. Why did his legs not give way? Bright lines of red drew themselves against the black skin of the creature's arm.

The historian's mouth opened. The pressure in his chest increased. And he knew this monster was clutching his still-throbbing heart.

SIETE

El Puño awoke. Before he opened his eyes, he could tell from the mixed smell of stale beer and cleanser he was in a bar. A few moments more, and he detected the heavy-air smells of exhaust, hot concrete and asphalt, the reek of feral dogs and garbage, and he knew he was in Mexico City.

Suddenly Beatriz appeared in his mind's eye. Sometimes that happened—inexplicably, when he wasn't thinking about her, and she looked exactly as she had when he last saw her…in Mexico City. Long black hair parted on the side; the quick smile that youth's delight with every surprise allowed. He opened and closed his hands, grasping nothing. The pain behind his sternum was the familiar one that greeted his every waking—a mixture of disappointment, guilt and grief. He opened his eyes. Sunlight came in a small barred window. He lay on a cot in a store room lined with beer kegs and liquor bottles. Clean clothes on a hanger hung from a nail sticking from a wooden shelf. He got up and dressed.

Through a curtained doorway and a small alcove stacked with odds and ends, then through a door that came out behind a bar. A young man came over and shook his hand. "Hey, El Puño de Bronce! It's me, Raoul, remember?"

The fighter stared at the young man several moments. Thick black hair brushed back from his face, an easy smile, denim jacket worn over a paisley shirt unbuttoned at the collar, a pair of faded jeans, and scuffed work boots. "Si," he answered.

Raoul led him around the bar to a table. "I'll bring out some breakfast. *Mi papa* said he saw you fight Jorge Gomez once, and you really clobbered him."

"That was a long time ago."

"Yeah, that's what he said." Raoul disappeared through another door, this one also in the back wall, but outside the bar. He returned with two plates of food, then retrieved a pot of coffee and a big mug from behind the bar.

"*Gracias.*"

"So why did you quit fighting?"

"Raoul!" A deep voice came from the doorway through which the young man had carried the food. "That's enough rude questions for our guest."

"Sorry, Papa."

A man came through the doorway to El Puño's table and extended his hand. "Ramon Andrade." He was a version of Raoul, twenty years older. His hair was a little thinner and threaded with gray, he was stout, and his legs bowed. A brash mustache covered his upper lip. "I see my brother-in-law's clothes fit you okay?"

El Puño patted his chest—he was dressed in a starched white

guyabera and tan slacks—and nodded. "*Muchas gracias.*"

Ramon sat at the table while El Puño continued eating. "He's a bigger fellow than me—big like you."

Raoul called out as he left through the saloon's front door: "Gotta go to work, Papa."

Ramon waved as El Puño said, "Thank you for your help!" He turned to Raoul's father. "Not everyone would have stopped for someone on the side of the road."

Ramon smiled. "He's a good boy." A clatter approached from the room behind the bar. "Here comes another one."

A ten-year-old version of Raoul burst into the room and flung himself into Ramon's arms. The man laughed and mussed the boy's hair. "This is Arturo, my youngest. Say hello to El Puño de Bronce."

"*Hola!*"

"*Hola,* Arturo!" El Puño smiled as he shook the boy's hand. Arturo squeezed tightly and shook with all his might. "Hey, that's quite a grip. Good thing I'll be retired by the time you're a luchador."

"Hah!" Arturo barked a laugh, then released his grip and stepped back to cling to his father's shoulder. "My papa says he saw you fight Gamma Gomez."

"That was a long time ago." El Puño smiled. "But I remember it took many days to wash off the green paint that rubbed off Gomez."

"You won the fight?"

"I think so."

"Why don't you fight anymore?"

"Arturo!" Ramon scolded.

The bell over the front door jangled. "Ah, here we go," Ramon said.

A feminine voice called out from behind El Puño. "Papa!"

A girl—El Puño corrected his first impression, *a young woman*—came from behind the fighter to hug Ramon and kiss his cheek. Her long black hair and flashing eyes—and something about the line of her jaw—marked her clearly as Ramon's daughter. Another young woman followed the first. She greeted Ramon respectfully, then the girls turned their eyes toward El Puño. They were both dressed in demure blouses and modest skirts.

Ramon introduced his daughter: "El Puño de Bronce, I am honored for you to meet my treasure, Valeria, and her friend Aura."

"Señoritas."

The young women said polite things until Valeria was interrupted by Arturo, who had been tugging at her sleeve since her arrival. The boy's sister swiftly turned and pinched his nose. Aura kept her widened eyes on El Puño.

"Valeria and Aura are students at the Universidad," Ramon bragged. He gave his daughter a stern look. "Why aren't you in class now?"

"Papa, we have class later. Profesor Vazquez invited us to El Museo Nacional de Antropología to see his new *momio!*"

"Eh?"

"It was in the papers!" Valeria poked Ramon's shoulder with her thumb. "Don't you read anything but your invoices?" She laughed and kissed him again.

Aura asked El Puño, "Did you hear about *el momio?*" The fighter hadn't seen the girl blink since she started staring at him.

"No, I've been, ah, I haven't seen the papers lately."

Aura continued staring. "We're going to go see it."

"So I hear."

"Before anyone else. The public, that is. The people who found it have seen it. And the museum workers." She nodded.

"I see."

"C'mon," Valeria said to Aura, "we should go. We don't want to be late to meet Profesor Vazquez." She tugged at her companion, who waved at El Puño as she was pulled away.

"Study well, girls," Ramon said.

"Goodbye, Treasure!" Arturo shouted.

The bell jangled and the door slammed shut. El Puño made a small smile. "You have raised your children well, Ramon."

"Ah, thank you, señor, but since their mother went to heaven, it is all thanks to God."

El Puño's smile disappeared. "What did God do that you didn't do, Ramon? Didn't you raise them, feed them, care for them, work for them?"

Shock widened Ramon's eyes. "Señor, don't you believe in God and His blessings?"

El Puño paused, and his gaze seemed to go elsewhere. "I believe in Hell."

Ramon crossed himself. He caught sight of Arturo standing at his shoulder. "Here," he said, and he took up El Puño's plates and handed them to the boy. "Take these to the kitchen. Wash them and the others."

Ramon watched his younger son disappear into the back, then turned to El Puño. "Señor…how can you say these things?"

El Puño stared at Ramon, who could see a bitter weariness in the eyes behind the mask.

"You know why I don't fight anymore?"

"Well," Ramon said, "I thought you retired. And then I read in the papers that you were fighting somebody in a village south of here. You were helping El Tigre Azul catch criminals."

"I was in the area," El Puño explained. "For years I got caught up fighting these crazy things. Witches. Monsters. I thought that's what I was supposed to do. Fight bad things, make them stop hurting people." He tilted his head back and forth and looked at his hands on the table. "But when there are bad things, there's usually something worse that's watching. Waiting." The ache from the morning pressed against his sternum again. He looked up at Ramon. "You ever hear of Mictlantecuhtli?"

Ramon shook his head.

"Lord of the underworld."

"Lord of the underworld?"

"The Aztec underworld," El Puño said. "Lord of Mictlan, the lowest hell in Hell, I guess you'd say."

"Aztec hell?" Confusion pulled furrows into Ramon's forehead.

"He was unhappy. I was fighting and beating his monsters. So he…"

Ramon waited a few moments before he asked, "Yes?"

"He...it stole away someone. A woman. Someone I love."

"What?"

But El Puño didn't hear. Instead, although his eyes stared at Ramon, he saw a bleak plain stretching before him—brownish-violet sand that crackled underfoot, interrupted by scrubby growths that showed no leaves but looked like writhing fingers of coral plucked from the ocean floor. The flatness gave way in places to great piles of fractured stone from which rang hoots and shrieks. The sky showed no moon, and what should have been glimmering stars were black cinders emanating a fierce cold. Structures stood in the distance—buildings the fighter had trekked to and then marveled at their construction from what appeared to be striated lengths of dinosaur bones.

El Puño blinked and again saw Ramon seated before him. The bar man's features were knotted in distress.

"He stole her. Beatriz," El Puño said. "And he grabs me somehow—hurls me into this hell and I try to find her, to bring her back. But all I find are monsters. I fight them, and then I'm thrown back here, to the world we know." His explanation lost its energy in its last few phrases, as though the fighter realized how foolish the words sounded, and as the grief that squeezed his heart thickened his throat.

"That's like Adán Luna!"

Both men jumped in their seats as the shout rang through the saloon. Ramon twisted in his chair and frowned at Arturo, who had been hiding by the bar and listening to El Puño's tale.

"Arturo!" Ramon said. "You are supposed to be in the kitchen!"

"Adán Luna!" Arturo repeated, ignoring his father. "Don't you know?" He dashed from the room, and less than a minute later returned. He held out a worn comic book for El Puño to see: Under the title *Titanes Planetarios* was a man in a bright red spacesuit firing a ray gun at a purple alien monster. The caption on the cover of the magazine identified the hero in the spacesuit as Adán Luna.

"The ray from the alien planet zaps Adán Luna and takes him from Earth," Arturo said breathlessly. "He goes to the planet and fights robots and mad scientists so he can smooch with his girl-friend. Then he gets zapped back home to Earth! He never knows when it's going to happen." Arturo grinned at El Puño, pleased for providing an explanation for the fighter's dilemma.

El Puño clapped the boy on the shoulder. "Thank you. That is very helpful."

Arturo beamed at his father. Ramon frowned, but Arturo chose to ignore this sign of disapproval. "I have to finish the dishes," the boy said before disappearing into the back.

Ramon stuttered in embarrassment. "El Puño, I am so sorry…"

The fighter waved away the words. "Don't be sorry, my friend. Arturo is like his brother and father—very helpful to those who clearly need help. No, I apologize for bringing my burden to you. You are gracious to a stranger who was spit from the earth, and you don't deserve to hear my worries." His mouth spread in a weary smile.

Ramon stared at El Puño before nodding. "All right. Please make yourself comfortable. I don't have much to offer, but consider this your home while you are in Mexico City. We live upstairs, over the bar, and there is room for your cot in Raoul's bedroom. We just couldn't get you up the stairs while you were…asleep."

"You are too, too kind."

"Eh, there is a rip in your mask. I have a sewing kit in the office," Ramon offered.

"*Muchas gracias.*"

El Puño watched Ramon go for the kit. He marveled at the good-ness of people. The fighter often felt as though he waded through a mire of bitterness. That strangers could be so kind was as wonderful and surprising to him as the crisp taste of cold water to a man lost in the desert.

OCHO

Valeria and Aura walked around the two chacmools near the door of the museum's exhibit preparation room. They were accompanied by one of the institution's docents, Geraldo. The museum's director—while gruff with his staff, he usually avoided all contact with the volunteers—had not informed the docents that both Profesor Vazquez and the new mummy were missing. So gray-haired, gangly old Geraldo—although he told the girls he hadn't seen their teacher—was charmed by their youth and enthusiasm, and thus led the pair to the prep room.

"No one is here," Aura said. She and Valeria surveyed the tools arranged on the tables and eyed the room's other contents. Both girls felt thrills crawling up their spines as they explored those parts of the museum rarely seen by the public.

Geraldo gestured. "The new mummy stuff is in the back there."

Valeria led the way. At the rear of the room, she gazed at the empty slab. She turned to Aura, then the young women scanned the shelves along the walls. "Where is it?" they asked simultaneously.

Valeria heard a noise from Geraldo. She looked back past Aura, then froze. Aura turned also and uttered a small squeak.

The old docent collapsed onto one of the preparer's tables, then slid to the floor, tools clattering around him. Standing over his humped form was a naked man. He was tall, and although his black skin was marked by creases and wrinkles, it shone under the lights. He was slender, but his muscles and strength were evident to the girls' eyes. His right arm was red to the elbow with blood that dripped in strings to the floor beside the unmoving Geraldo.

Valeria could not move. She couldn't stop staring at the man as he strode toward her and Aura, so she was unable to turn and see her companion's reaction. She heard Aura's labored breathing—almost a panting—and then Valeria grew aware she, also, was fighting for air.

As the black figure approached, she saw his green eyes. They seemed to glow, and the other colors in the room faded until everything was a pale green—everything except the man's ebony skin.

He stopped before Aura. Valeria saw his right hand rise—still bloody, the fingers straight and close together, like a blade—and then the hand darted from her sight. She heard a chunk, like a shovel chopping into earth, and a gasp. Valeria tried unsuccessfully to turn her head. Aura's voice made little noises, like a frightened kitten.

In a corner of her mind, Valeria's consciousness tried to shrink and hide. She began to pray: *"Padre nuestro, que estás en el cielo. Santificado sea tu nombre. Venga tu reino."*

Valeria heard slicing and sucking noises, and Aura's kitten sounds changed to a low gurgling. Still Valeria could see only the black, expressionless face of the man who stood before the two girls. The images she saw began to strobe as her panic ratcheted upward. Her heart hammered in her ears at an impossible pace. She wondered if the rush of adrenaline was making her delusional, because the man's face seemed to change shape as he put the bloody hand to his mouth. It held a fist-sized, scarlet thing that steamed and dripped crimson, and the man's jaws distended as he chomped into it like Valeria would bite into an apple.

She heard a sound like a sack of grain dropping to the pavement. Valeria no longer sensed Aura standing beside her. Instead, she felt a cold emptiness.

The thing—Valeria could no longer think of it as a man—licked its fingers. It stood right in front of the young woman.

Stress constricted Valeria's sight. She saw only the creature's glowing green eyes and its mouth in terrible detail. Its black chin dripped blood. Each drop wavered, caught the light in a glistening crescent, then fell. Valeria could hear it strike the floor—*spat!*—somehow, impossibly, over the pounding of her pulse in her ears.

The thing extended its hand. It held its palm open over Valeria's left breast. It did not touch her, but her flesh chilled at the nearness of its hand. Its head tilted slightly to its right. Then she saw its lips curl and ripple like the petals of a flower moved by the wind. Her legs could not hold her erect any longer, but the creature's power kept her from falling. Valeria waited for its hand to strike her, and a piercing keening filled her ears.

Then the thing spoke: a slow, ugly sound like a stone dragged over gravel. The green of its eyes grew brighter as it said in Spanish, *"Una virgen."*

NUEVE

The contemporary architecture of El Museo was meant to represent a Mexico that embraced its past while looking to the future. But based on what El Puño de Bronce had heard on the radio in Raoul's truck, the past had a throttle hold on the present.

After his conversation with Ramon, El Puño had carried his cot upstairs to the family's home. He had sat in a rocking chair by a window, where he had repaired the tears in his mask and then lazed like a cat. He had foolishly dared to believe he had earned a rest, that misfortune had released him awhile.

Then he had heard the heartbroken wailing from downstairs. He had gone into Ramon's saloon, where the bar owner had turned a desperate expression his way while comforting another man. "This is Aura's father," Ramon said. "They found her body. She is dead. Dead! At the museum!"

El Puño stared at Ramon a moment, stunned. "Valeria? Where is she?"

"I—I don't know. No one knows. She wasn't there." Ramon's eyes seemed to look past El Puño to something only he could see. The fighter noticed Arturo clinging to his father's pants leg, crying. Aura's father had his head on the bar and had covered his face with his arms. His back shook with sobbing, and Ramon's arm rested across the man's shoulders.

The bar's patrons stared, unmoving, at the strange tableau.

Raoul rushed in. "Papa! I heard on the radio!"

"Raoul!" El Puño snapped. "Take me to the museum. Now!"

During the ride, the radio announcer sounded nearly hysterical. His breathless recounting made El Puño repeatedly clench and relax his fists on his knees.

"At least eight bodies have been found in the basement of El Museo Nacional de Antropología," the announcer said. "They include those of museum staff and Profesor Jorge Vazquez, celebrated for his archaeological work. He had been named to work on the recently discovered mummy, which is missing, according to the museum's director."

106

Ramon and his family, El Puño thought. They brought me into their home and cared for me, and my presence has cursed them.

Raoul's truck was still rolling in front of the museum when El Puño leapt out. He pushed through the newspaper and radio people thronged at the entrance. One of the police recognized the fighter from previous exploits and waved him inside.

The preparation room was crowded—with detectives and corpses, along with the museum's tools and exhibits waiting for repair and presentation. El Puño stepped past a chacmool by the entrance and surveyed the activity. Near the back of the room were piled the bodies of the dead. A detective, who introduced himself as Gomez, identified each for him: "Profesor Vazquez. His assistant, Oscar Peña. A museum guard, Ricardo Ramirez. Jaime Guerrero, maintenance man. Juan Montez, private detective. Gabriel Lopez, archaeologist. Geraldo Gutierrez, volunteer. Aura Flores, student. Hearts carved out, every one." Gomez was beefy. He was stylishly dressed in a yellow suit—like a TV detective. He tried to act tough, but his face was pale.

"Another girl, Valeria Andrade," El Puño said. "She was with Aura this morning."

Gomez gestured loosely with his arm. "This is all we have. It's enough."

Blood covered the floor. El Puño stepped around the crimson pool to look at the carved slab, surrounded by blood like a horrific moat.

"The mummy came on that, according to the director," Gomez said. "Apparently it's been missing as long as Vazquez."

"Where did these bodies come from?" El Puño asked. "Where were they hidden that a janitor just found them today?"

Gomez stood in place, but turned a circle to take in the entire room. "Good question."

A photographer whose flash bulbs had filled the room with periodic bursts of white called from the door. "Hey, Gomez, I'm heading back to the station. I got shots of everything." Gomez waved. Other technicians huddled over tables and the floor, dusting for prints, scrutinizing every square inch for clues.

El Puño cleared his throat. "Can you thin this crowd? I'd like to take a look around on my own."

Gomez stared, then nodded. "Sure." He shooed everyone else out of the room, then rejoined El Puño after he closed the door. "Okay."

The fighter walked the edges of the room several minutes. Then he stopped by the chacmool near the door. "Hey," he said. El Puño tapped a finger between the carved figure's eyes. "Wake up."

After a few moments, the statue's eyes slowly blinked with a sound like sheets of sandpaper rubbed together. The thing moved its jaws, then said, "*Hola.*"

Gomez staggered back and nearly fell onto the jumble of dead bodies. "*Mierda!*"

"Yeah," El Puño said. "Hang out with enough ghosts and witches, weird stuff from the Dread World rubs off. I can communicate with its denizens—*un poco*—sometimes."

"D-Dread World?" Gomez stared at the chacmool, which twisted its head from side to side like an old man with a kink in his neck.

"Where all the bad things live," El Puño said. "Another dimension, I guess. Another world. Full of supernatural bad stuff, everything the pagans loved. Just one invisible door away from us at all times." He glanced at Gomez. "Makes Mexico City air smell like a bouquet."

"I know you," the chacmool spoke with its raspy voice. "El Puño de Bronce. Everybody in *el mundo temor* knows you."

"Yeah, yeah, like a radio wave connecting everything connected to the Dread World," El Puño said. "I've heard it before.

Gomez pointed. "It speaks Spanish!"

"Sit around for hundreds of years, you listen. Learn a few things," the chacmool said. "Did you know Motecuhzoma—well, Montezuma to you—had terrible gas? Whew."

"That's enough," the fighter said. "Where's *la momia?* Where is the girl, Valeria?"

"I don't know. But I can show you where they went."

El Puño eyed the stone figure a moment before answering. "All right."

The chacmool slowly rose from its reclining position. It stood a head taller than El Puño. "Oh, that's good." It took an unsteady step forward, then another. Each movement sounded like two bricks rubbed together. It walked toward the back of the room. Gomez pressed his back against a wall and crossed himself.

Reaching the middle of the prep room, the chacmool took a swing at El Puño, lightning fast. The fighter ducked, snatched up a five-pound sledge from a shelf. Before the chacmool could swing around again, El Puño rapped the mallet against the figure's head. The chacmool staggered back a step. "Hey!" it complained. "I'm a valuable antiquity."

"You're a smart-ass rock. Maybe a future pile of gravel," El Puño answered. "I've dealt with chacmools before. You're tricky. I'll keep my eye on you and this hammer in my hand. Act right and show me the mummy."

The chacmool muttered, but continued past the pile of bodies and stood near a side wall. "Here," it said. It tapped the wall with both hands. The paint seemed to flake from the wall and then melt, revealing a gaping hole. Beyond was blackness.

"What's that?" Gomez asked.

El Puño shook his head. "Tunnels. Mexico City is built on ages of previous cities. This is something under the city built who-knows-when."

"Templo Mayor," the chacmool said. Gomez heard something in the thing's voice that chilled the back of his neck.

"Okay, back to your seat," El Puño ordered.

"Aw, come on. I know more stuff. Hernán Cortés must never have taken off that cuirass for a bath, let me tell you. And—"

"Shut up," El Puño said.

The chacmool abruptly stuck its head into the wall's opening and whispered several moments. Then it came back into the room. As it settled back into its original reclining position, El Puño asked, "What were you doing at that hole?"

"Sending you a message," it answered. "You'll hear it when you catch up to it."

109

"Great," the fighter sighed. "Go back to sleep."

Gomez marveled. He could see the chacmool was again an inanimate object. He turned to the hole in the wall. "What is this? Where'd it come from?"

El Puño shrugged and tossed a flashlight to the detective. "Magic hole, I guess. I don't like mummies. I don't like chacmools. But we have to find Valeria."

Both men directed beams of light into the darkness as they stepped through the gap. They were in a low, narrow tunnel. "Here," Gomez said, aiming his lamp on the rubble-strewn floor. A wide puddle reflected a dull shine. "The bodies weren't found because they were hidden here."

"Guess he tossed them back into the prep room when he cleared out with Valeria."

"Who?"

"*La momia.*"

Gomez stared at El Puño. "You think a dead thing killed those people? Took the girl?"

El Puño continued deeper into the passage as he spoke. "You just saw a statue walk and talk, right?"

Gomez sputtered. "Maybe—maybe that chacmool killed those people."

"No, it couldn't move until I woke it up. I think it was the mummy."

Gomez could voice no reply. He simply followed the fighter; there wasn't enough room for them to walk abreast.

The low confines of the tunnel—its smell of garbage and earthen rot—brought to El Puño's mind his excursions to the Dread World, to the hell over which Mictlantecuhtli ruled. The darkness and chill of the passage seemed to taint El Puño's blood. The familiar pain at his breast bone reappeared. He had failed his Beatriz. He could not let a monster have Valeria. He could not let his curse break Ramon Andrade's heart.

He put aside these thoughts. Dwelling on Beatriz was flirting with despair. He could not give in to darkness. Doing so would mean he would fail everyone.

"Here!" Gomez said. He lifted something from the floor, brought it into the light beam. A woman's shoe.

"Must be hers," El Puño said.

They crawled over piles of rubble, kicked aside rats. The path turned one way for yards, then another. Water dripped into foul puddles. They came to a dead end.

Gomez turned his light this way and that. "Did we turn the wrong way?"

El Puño studied the heap of earth and broken stones that clogged the passage. "No, here." His light surrounded a bloody hand print. "It did this to stop us. Come on."

He began to push aside rocks and loose dirt. He tilted a large slab that rolled past Gomez and thudded to the floor. They shoved, scooped and scraped. Finally they cleared a hole big enough for El Puño to thrust his broad shoulders through.

"Come on."

Gomez scrambled through the gap and followed.

Their lamps darted against the dark. Finally the tunnel opened into what had been a vast plaza. Now hidden from the sun, it was roofed by the strata from years of the city overhead being built and rebuilt, layer upon layer. Massive piles of debris and crumbled structures acted as piers supporting the muck-dripping ceiling.

The men advanced slowly. "Listen," whispered Gomez.

A murmuring. Whimpering. Not too distant.

El Puño began to run. Gomez trailed, panting. Behind a mass of rubble they found a weird figure—tall, naked, emaciated but sinewy—standing over the supine Valeria. Her eyes were open, staring at the creature, but she appeared unable to move. The thing—clearly the reanimated mummy—had one arm raised. It held a long blade that looked like one of several ceremonial daggers El Puño had seen in the prep room.

The fighter bounded toward the pair. He leaped over Valeria and slammed head-first into the mummy's solar plexus. The two tumbled among the scattered stones on the floor as the mummy dropped the knife.

"Get her out of here!" El Puño shouted to Gomez. While the detective helped the limp girl to her feet, El Puño scrabbled in the debris for the dagger. He spotted the distinctive Aztec inscriptions on the blade and grabbed the hilt. He spun around, the knife point extended. The creature was swift—it was almost upon him. The dagger slashed through its torso, and the mummy staggered back.

The sliced black flesh gaped open. Inside the wound were thick, pale bristles turned inward.

The chacmool's grating whisper came to El Puño's ear then: "Your mummy is a shape changer."

El Puño swore. "I hate shape changers."

DIEZ

The gash in the mummy's torso closed like a mouth, then sealed, as if the blade had never touched it.

El Puño threw himself at the creature. He wasn't impossibly mighty like the costumed heroes in *comiquitas,* but he was stronger and tougher than most men. He didn't know if this came from his frequent forays into the Dread World—a side effect, like his ability to interact with the chacmool—or if Mictlantecuhtli had cursed him in this fashion as a way to make his failures even more frustrating.

The fighter held the mummy in a bear hug. The monster snarled and swatted his face and arms repeatedly. All the while, the chacmool's irritating whisper continued: "Not just any shape changer, El Puño—but a *jaguar humanizado,* a were-jaguar. Worshipped by the Olmec, the mother culture for all Mesoamerica."

"Shut up," El Puño said, but he knew the chacmool had sent his whisper ahead before the fighter and Gomez had entered the tunnels.

El Puño grappled with the mummy as it writhed and slid from his grasp. One of its glossy black arms grew impossibly long and circled his throat. El Puño began to fight for air. He slammed his fists into the creature's sternum and abdomen. The chacmool's disembodied voice kept hissing in his ears: "The Aztecs thought he

112

was just another blood-letter. The other priests were jealous of his celebrity. They tried to assassinate him—and discovered his secret. He was older than their civilization."

El Puño stabbed his fingers into the mummy's eyes. It gasped and released him. The fighter heaved air into his lungs as he staggered back.

"They could not kill El Jaguar," the chacmool continued. "They used magic to bind him to the slab. It was covered with incantations to hold him forever. But the stone was cracked on its way to the museum. The spell was weakened. The mummy got free."

The mummy's hand slashed out, and its black fingernails left four slices in El Puño's shirt. Blood began to run down his chest.

"Good luck, El Puño," the chacmool grated. "You may never find your Beatriz now."

El Puño rushed the creature and slammed against its legs. The tackle brought the monster to the floor. It kicked El Puño's head and chest and growled. The fighter rolled. The mummy slashed at him with its talons. Torn and bleeding, El Puño pushed inside the thing's whipping arms and smashed a fist into the mummy's throat.

The monster hacked and gagged. Its chest heaved. Then the mummy's face began to change—its jaw elongated and a cleft appeared at the top of its head. Its eyes started to glow green.

El Puño knew he had to stop this thing now. If the mummy changed to its jaguar aspect, he was done for.

The fighter grabbed the monster's shoulders and twisted. He tumbled over and threw the mummy onto its face. El Puño slammed his knees into the creature's spine, then dropped so that he was seated on the mummy's lower back. He grabbed the creature's arms and pulled back so the thing's armpits rested on his raised thighs. While the mummy snarled and kicked to throw El Puño off, the fighter reached around both sides of the monster's head and laced his fingers together under its chin. He pulled backward.

El Puño had the mummy in a *quebradora de a caballo* hold—painful and disorienting. The fighter pulled harder, not letting up. The creature gurgled, its snarls trapped in its throat as its neck and spine bent backward, the angle more acute with each moment.

El Puño's arms swelled with his exertion. His hands were slick with blood, but he would not relent. The mummy thrashed under him. The fighter took a deep breath, and as he exhaled and heaved backward, the cavern echoed with a grinding *crack!*

El Puño fell back. The mummy's head was in his hands, its teeth snapping. But the glow was fading from its eyes.

The fighter looked at the monster's headless neck. Gouts of blood rushed out—not just the blood of the creature's recent victims, but that of centuries' worth of sacrifices. The corpse quivered and hopped about as the scarlet flood covered the stone-scattered floor.

El Puño dashed the mummy's head against a large rock. The skull shattered and then burst into a cloud of dust that floated a moment on the crimson surface of the spreading pool, then sank.

Blood continued to gush from the neck of the corpse. El Puño stood in a scarlet lake already three inches deep in this vast cavern, and the flood showed no signs of stopping. As the fighter headed toward the tunnel to follow the trail Gomez had taken Valeria, the mummy's body was covered by the red flow. More blood continued to spew up and disturb the pool's surface.

El Puño snatched up his light where it had fallen. As he headed back to the museum, he whispered: "I hate shape changers."

EPILOG
The Dread World

In a place filled with flickering lights with no apparent source, a place where the darkness had a suffocating presence, the thing that had been the were-jaguar mummy was pinioned by many hands. It groaned.

It was held by a single human-faced creature painted black, red and yellow in ceremonial Aztec designs. The thing clutching the mummy had more than a dozen arms; no body—the shoulders of the arms all melded in a knot where the chest and abdomen should have been. It stood on two arms, using hands instead of feet. With the sounds of sucking swamp muck and grinding gristle, the thing's hands tore the mummy's arms from its shoulders. Its hands ripped the mummy's legs from its pelvis. Its thumbs dug into the mummy's eye sockets and wrenched the Olmec's head from its neck.

Another creature—made of many legs, like a squirming nest of snakes—whirled about the chamber and stamped the mummy's discarded limbs with its many feet. Still another creature—made of teeth like a tumbleweed of tangled ivory—bit and chewed the limbs after they were flattened by the flailing legs.

As the mummy was torn and beaten, its missing limbs and head would regrow in a moment, to be wrenched apart again.

The creature of many arms said, "Welcome to the lowest hell of Hell. Lord Mictlantecuhtli thanks you for your great service. You have filled his hell with many slaves. You have his undying love."

And the creature ripped another arm from the mummy's shoulder.

THE WARRIOR AND THE STONE

by John C. Bruening

Jason Bennett raised his binoculars and scanned the mountain path ahead of him, following it with his eyes to its natural ending point. The distance was no more than a half mile, but that half mile was an uphill slope of rock, covered with just enough snow and ice to make it interesting. It was a difficult stretch made even more challenging by biting cold air and a persistent wind.

To make matters worse, it was getting dark. He would need to cover the distance quickly if he hoped to reach his destination by nightfall.

That destination was the cave at the end of the path. Bennett examined the entrance to the cavern through the binoculars. It wasn't much to look at—a relatively small, gaping hole in the rock wall, leading to a place devoid of what little light the heavily clouded late-day sky had to offer.

In fact, the mouth of the cave was so nondescript and unremarkable that Bennett began to doubt the validity of the sketchy information that had brought him to this place. His journey had taken him halfway around the world, and it included a highly unorthodox—not to mention illegal—foray behind the Iron Curtain, all the way through Eastern Europe and across the Taklamakan Desert in the northwest corner of China. Along the way, he had little more than an ancient tale of a seventh-century Chinese warrior and a crude map to guide him to the warrior's final resting place in the nineteen-hundred-mile expanse of the Kunlun Mountains.

It was September, a time of year when conditions in the upper tier of the Kunlun weren't necessarily life threatening yet, but they weren't exactly comfortable either. There wasn't much direct sunlight amid the heavy cloud cover of the last few days, but visible or not, the sun would be completely below the horizon in less than three hours. At that point, the temperature would drop into the twenties, and the wind would make things much colder still.

While Bennett was looking up the mountain path and pondering climate and terrain, another man standing some twenty feet away from him had his binoculars trained in the opposite direction.

"It will be many hours, Mr. Jake," said the second man, addressing Bennett by the nickname he'd earned many years earlier. "But there is no question that our friends will be here. It would be best if we move quickly to the cave, find what we seek—if there is anything there to be found—and move on."

This second man—somewhat smaller than Bennett, with dark hair and intelligent eyes—was Haluk, one of the most reliable travel guides on either side of the Iron Curtain. A native of Turkey, Haluk spoke fluent English and four other languages that Bennett knew of—and probably a couple more that he didn't know of. Not quite thirty years old, Haluk had spent his relatively short lifetime developing an uncanny knowledge of mountain and desert geography throughout Europe and the Soviet Union. His knowledge had been a valuable resource to Bennett on more than one prior occasion.

Haluk's mention of "friends" was strictly a euphemism. A little more than two miles behind them to the west, a team of Soviet and Chinese operatives made their way through the same mountain pass that he and Bennett had been covering for the past three days. Based on intelligence he had spent months cobbling together—from countless hours of broadcasts from Radio Free Europe and other shortwave channels, along with information from his vast network of connections in the European and Soviet underground—Haluk had had learned that the operatives were on a mission whose objective was two-fold.

First and foremost, they had been charged by the Kremlin and the defense ministry of Communist China to scout the mountain range for a suitable place to build a missile base. There were currently holes in the Soviet armor when it came to certain European nations and the British Isles, all of whom had developed nuclear capabilities just a few years earlier. The extra fire power in the mountains of China would strengthen military leverage against the West.

But deeper intelligence from Haluk's network suggested an additional objective, and a less official one. The Chinese had been made aware of the existence of a specific treasure hidden somewhere in the mountains—something of great historical and cultural significance—and it so happened that it was the very same item that Bennett himself had come halfway around the word to find.

The race through the mountains may have been a slow one, but it was a race just the same—and both runners in the contest were seeking the same prize.

"Can you tell how many?" said Bennett.

Haluk kept staring through the binoculars. "Four," he said after a moment. "No, not four. Five."

"The question is," Bennett muttered, "can they see us?"

"That is a question I cannot answer, Mr. Jake," said Haluk. "There are fewer of us than there are of them. So perhaps we are harder to see at this distance. It may be that they do not see us because they are not looking for us."

Bennett had known Haluk too long and too well not to trust his information or his instincts. Two miles was a long way in a mountain pass, about a day's journey, but if the Turk said the team of operatives was headed their way, the team was definitely headed their way.

~ ~ ~

On flatter terrain, in better weather, a half-mile hike to a cave would have taken them ten or fifteen minutes. In these mountains under these conditions, it took them a little more than an hour and a half. Along the way, Bennett's internal struggle to balance hope against skepticism grew increasingly intense.

And the external conditions didn't help much. The combination of the heavy packs on their backs and the thin air of the mountain altitude forced them to stop to rest at the halfway mark.

Haluk slid his pack off his shoulders and rested it on the ground. "All this way," he said, exhaling deeply and parking his backside on a large, flat stone, "for a piece of jade."

The same thought had been nagging at Bennett for the better part of an hour, but he'd been doing his best to suppress the doubt. "Well, according to the legend, the Stone of Immortality is much more than that," he said, dropping his own pack and taking a seat on a nearby stone. "The Chinese have considered jade a life-giving substance for thousands of years, but this particular stone was believed to be something much more than that. It was believed to have the power to restore life to the dead and preserve it indefinitely."

Haluk flexed his shoulders and rolled his neck. "But this is 1960," he said. "This is the age of spacecraft and science. You, an American, should understand this better than anyone—with your handsome young senator who seeks to lead the free world with his talk of new frontiers. Surely, you cannot believe in such things as ancient stones with magical powers."

The Turk turned and looked further up the path toward the cave, which was now only about a quarter-mile from where they were sitting. "And how can we even know if this is the right path to the right cave?" He looked back at Bennett. "Indeed, how can we even know if this is the right mountain?"

Bennett sighed. "Have I ever mentioned how good your English is?"

"Yes. Every time we argue."

Both men were silent for a minute or two. Without the packs, without the fight against the steep grade of the path, their breath eventually settled into something less labored and more even. The hoods of their parkas fluttered as a cold wind—light but persistent—whistled along the mountain range.

Haluk broke the silence. "You have paid me well for my services on this adventure, as you always do," he said. "But you have told me little."

"I've told you little because I'm fairly certain that an American and a European snooping around the mountains of Communist China without the proper papers is a violation of international law. So if we find ourselves in a jam with Interpol or the Chinese Ministry or the KGB or whoever else, the less you know, the less trouble you can get into."

Haluk shrugged. "What trouble could we possibly get into?" he said, his voice thick with mock innocence. "If we just tell them we're chasing a magic stone from a thirteen-hundred-year-old legend, I'm sure they will understand."

Bennett shook his head. "I don't know about legends," he said. "But I do know about history."

"Tell me," said Haluk.

"I'm sure you're familiar with some of it," said Bennett. "For centuries, all the way up until a decade ago, China and Tibet were two distinct sovereign entities. These mountains were the dividing line between the powerful Tibetan Empire to the south and the Taklamakan Desert to the north. In the seventh century, there were several individual territories—oasis states—along the north side of the mountain range. One of the most prosperous of these was the Kingdom of Khotan. It was located along one branch of the Spice Roads, the trade routes that snaked across Asia and into Europe. Khotan was also important because it was one of four Chinese military garrisons positioned along the mountains to protect against invaders."

"The Spice Roads," Haluk said, his face twisting into a wry grin. "History is always the same, everywhere in the world. History is what happens at the place where geography and commerce cross paths."

Bennett chuckled. He couldn't dispute Haluk's plain-spoken wisdom.

"It is not so hard to think of China and Tibet as two separate entities, once upon a time," said Haluk. "One is on a high plateau that overlooks the basin of the other."

"They were very different cultures," said Bennett, "and they didn't get along very well."

Haluk shrugged. "Mao has tried to unite them by claiming Tibet as part of his People's Republic of China," he said, "and yet they still do not get along. Just look at the events of a year ago, with the Chinese military occupying the region and killing tens of thousands of Tibetans in an uprising."

Bennett knew Haluk understood political upheaval better than most, and on a first-hand basis. His own homeland of Turkey had undergone a military coup just months earlier. Indeed, finding Haluk amid the turmoil and enlisting his services for this expedition had been no easy task—a seemingly endless series of secret communications with a list of contacts a mile long.

"Well, things weren't much better between the Tibetans and the Chinese thirteen-hundred years ago, when it was Tibet that was the aggressor nation," said Bennett. "The Tibetan emperor at the time was an expansionist. He sent bands of raiders north over these mountains and into Chinese territory on the other side. They went into places like Khotan and other oasis states along the mountain border."

"Khotan," said Haluk. "That was the place where you found the scroll and the map."

"Well, yes and no. Khotan hasn't existed for centuries. But I was not far from here several months ago with a team from the university. We were digging at the foot of these mountains, at the ruins of a Buddhist temple that had been at the heart of Khotan. We found a scroll in an underground vault beneath the place where the temple had stood. The scroll said the temple had housed a secret chamber where the monks kept what they called the búxiǔ shítou—the Stone of Immortality."

Bennett reached for his canteen and took a gulp of water. "Based on the account in the scroll, combined with what we already know from history, it's not hard to piece together the scenario," he said, closing up the canteen and returning it to his backpack. "With the Tibetan Empire pushing into the south, it was just a matter of time before they heard about the stone, and the emperor promised a generous reward for whoever would take it from the temple and bring it back to him."

He traced the remaining stretch of the path with his naked eyes. He no longer needed the binoculars.

"And if the legend is to be believed," he went on, "a band of raiders accepted the emperor's challenge. The scroll told the story of an attack by Tibetan invaders. According to the accounts, there were six of them. They stormed the temple in Khotan, outnumbering the outer guards and easily overpowering them. There were two more guards inside, the last line of defense protecting the stone in a room shrouded in darkness."

Haluk looked at him quizzically. "Why darkness?"

"According to the legend, the stone was believed to be sensitive to light. It was believed that direct sunlight would awaken its powers of reanimation."

Haluk shrugged and raised his eyes to the sky. "Well, magic or not, there is not much chance of such a thing happening here. I do not think the sun has broken through these clouds in at least five days."

Bennett looked up to the sky himself. "It's typical in these mountains," he said. "I'm no meteorologist, but the weather patterns between the plateau to the south and the lowlands to the north usually make for long stretches of heavy cloud cover."

After a moment, he took a deep breath and pushed himself up from the rock. "Alright, come on," he said, reaching for his backpack. "It's getting dark quickly. Let's keep moving."

Both men hoisted their packs. After a few adjustments to their harnesses, they were back on the path.

They climbed a bit further in silence, until Haluk spoke. "So what happened in this temple?"

"All of the guards were wiped out except for one," said Bennett.

"A warrior named Shi Zhu. He took the stone from its chamber and fled. The scroll says he headed for the mountains, to a secret place known only to the monks. It was a place where they went to fast and meditate and pray—and obviously a place to hide when threats became too dangerous."

Bennett adjusted a strap on his backpack to relieve some of the pressure on his shoulder. "The last person he spoke to was a Buddhist monk who encouraged him to take the stone and get to a safe place," he went on. "It was the monk who authored the scroll and told the story of the battle in the temple and the brave warrior who guarded the stone with his life and took it with him into the mountains to keep it protected and out of the wrong hands."

The Turk flashed the wry smile again. "Tell me, Mr. Jake: Do you believe any of this?"

"Haluk, this job isn't about what I believe," said Bennett. "It's about what I find from the past and how it can bring clarity to the present."

Like a long-distance runner, he felt a surge of untapped energy as they covered the last two- or three-hundred yards to the cave. He was no more sure of the accuracy of his instincts than he was several hundred miles ago, but he had come this far. He had to see it through.

And if nothing else, he was close to exhaustion. A chance to rest—even for just an hour—would feel almost as valuable right now as the discovery of a priceless Chinese artifact.

They came to a stop about twenty feet from the mouth of the cave.

"Maybe this is where we learn where the legend ends and the truth begins," said Bennett.

~ ~ ~

They stepped into the shadowy space and immediately dug into their packs for their flashlights. After no more than a couple steps, it was apparent to both men that navigating the interior terrain would be tricky. The floor was covered with stalagmites and other uneven rock formations, which forced them to move slowly and carefully.

They were no more than forty feet beyond the entrance when they came to a smaller passage that branched off to the right. Both men aimed their flashlight beams into the yawning blackness of the side passage, creating odd, dancing shadows along the inner walls beyond.

Bennett glanced at Haluk. "I'll keep following this main passage," he said. "You take a look in that secondary branch. Don't go too far in, and be careful."

Haluk nodded, following his own beam and steering himself to the right, toward the side passage. Along the way, he stepped gingerly over and across the uneven floor.

Bennett kept moving through the main passageway. After a couple minutes, he came upon a space glowing with a dim but unmistakable light from a source other than his flashlight. He stopped and swept the area with his beam and determined that the floor in this space was much more even than it had been in the space he and Haluk had covered since they entered the cave. Not perfectly smooth by any means, but much flatter than elsewhere.

He traced the perimeter of the flat space with his flashlight beam and realized that it was roughly oval-shaped. In the center of the space was a large rectangular stone slab propped up on either side by two equally large blocks of stone.

Unlike everything else around them, these stones weren't part of any natural formations. The surfaces were too smooth, the angles too precise. These large stones were purposefully cut and arranged, although by whom—or when—was beyond anything Bennett could surmise. And how they were brought into this space at this height in the mountains was even harder to imagine.

At the very least, the arrangement of the three stones amounted to a large table. But Bennett suspected it was something more than that.

It was an altar.

And above this altar was an opening in the ceiling of the cave that allowed in natural light from the outside. It wasn't much illumination—especially given the cloud cover and the time of day—but it allowed light into the chamber from a place other than Bennett's flashlight.

Bennett stared at all of it—the stone altar positioned carefully on an even stretch of floor beneath the naturally occurring aperture above—for nearly a full minute. He was vaguely aware that his breath was coming shorter and faster than it had been a few minutes earlier. He felt as though he needed to convince himself that he was indeed seeing what he thought he was seeing. In the end, there was no mistaking what he was looking at.

"Haluk!" Bennett called. "Come and take a look at this!"

Bennett kept his eyes trained on the altar as he listened to Haluk's movement in the distance. He heard to the quickening of the Turk's footfalls, despite the uneven terrain inside the cave. Within a minute, Haluk came up behind Bennett.

"What is it?" asked the guide. "What have you…?" But his question choked off as he came up behind Bennett and stepped around his shoulder.

"Mr. Jake," he whispered, eyes wide and mouth agape.

"My God, Haluk," Bennett said breathlessly. "This is it. The Window to the Heavens, just like the legend says. We're in the mountain temple."

"But the question still remains," said Haluk, "is the rest of the legend true? Of all the countless caves of all the countless mountains of the Kunlun, did Shi Zhu come here to escape the Tibetan marauders? And if so, did he bring the Stone of Immortality with him?"

They stepped closer to the oval shaped space and the stone altar positioned in the middle of it. Bennett ran his hand along the smooth horizontal surface of the top stone, and likewise touched the two stones underneath that supported it on either side. He looked closely at the surface of each for carvings of any kind, but found none.

"Look here," said Haluk, interrupting his concentration. Bennett turned toward the guide and saw that he was about thirty feet away, crouched in a corner located deeper into the chamber. He was directing his flashlight beam with one hand and pointing with the other.

Bennett crossed the space of the chamber and came up beside Haluk, who had trained his flashlight beam on a few objects positioned randomly on the cave floor. Bennett scanned the objects with his own flashlight and recognized a sword, a rectangular shield and a five-foot length of carved wooden staff.

Bennett kept scanning until his beam stopped at what appeared to be the remains of a large mountain animal. He stepped forward to get a better look, and realized that the remains were partially embedded in the rock formations along the space were the cave wall met the floor.

Haluk had stepped up alongside Bennett and trained his flashlight beam on the animal remains. "I don't understand," he said. "Whatever that thing is, how was it trapped inside the rock?"

"It makes sense," said Bennett, glancing up at the cave ceiling. "That's what happens over the course of centuries in a place like this. Rock formations build up along the floor, created by mineral deposits dripping off the ceiling and solidifying over time."

He tapped a knuckle against one of the taller stalagmites a few inches from his knee. "That's where these things come from," he said, noting how hard and unforgiving the formation felt against the bony curl of his finger. "The layers build upward to create spike formations, like inverted icicles—only made out of minerals rather than ice."

Bennett continued to scan the space near the animal carcass and noticed what appeared to be oil lamps made from clay. He knelt down and carefully moved the lamps aside. He reached out and touched the outstretched paw of the dead thing.

And then he realized that the limb was not a paw at all. It was something else entirely. Though desiccated over time into something hard, lean and leathery, Bennett knew exactly what it was.

"My God," he whispered. "This is a human hand."

Haluk let out a small gasp, but Bennett barely heard it. The archaeologist had already unslung his backpack and begun rummaging inside it.

"These remains," said Bennett, his breath short and words coming fast. "This is a man, partially wrapped in an animal skin. Whoever he is—or whoever he was—he probably wrapped himself in the pelt to keep himself warm."

"Do you think—?"

Bennett cut Haluk off before he could ask the question. "Get some of your tools out," he said, still digging into his own backpack. "We need to see if we can clear away some of the rock and dig this... this thing out."

Within thirty seconds, they were both chipping and scraping at the stone formations around the pelt and the remains inside it. They worked silently for several minutes, taking care not to damage the exposed portions. Progress was slow, but after nearly a half hour, most of the body had been uncovered. While Bennett felt a growing sense of anticipation, Haluk's face belied something entirely different.

"Mr. Jake," the Turk said, checking the illuminated dial of his watch and glancing back toward the cave entrance, "I know this is an important discovery, but I am concerned that the longer we stay here, the closer our friends will be to catching up with us."

Bennett glanced back toward the entrance himself. "It'll be okay," he said, but with only a partial degree of certainty. "I'm sure they've made camp for the night. The sun's almost completely down. Traveling through mountain terrain in these conditions is just too risky in the dark. They won't be on the move again until sunrise."

They kept digging, forcing themselves to maintain a light hand and chip away at only small portions of rock at a time, so as not to damage the remains. Restraint was a challenge for Bennett, who was getting a clearer sense with each passing minute of exactly what—and who—they had discovered.

After another twenty minutes, they had broken through several layers of mineral and rock, enough to get a closer look at the torso of the figure that had been well preserved in the cold mountain air. Bennett used a small brush to clear away some last bits of dust and debris, and slowly peeled away the remaining fragments of the animal skin.

And there, tied around its neck with a leather thong and resting on its chest, was a chunk of jade about the size and shape of a robin's egg.

The legend was true. Shi Zhu, the Chinese warrior, had escaped to the mountain temple thirteen-hundred years ago, and Bennett and Haluk had found him. They had found the Stone of Immortality.

Bennett reached down and took the stone in his hand, taking care not to break or damage the strip of leather that held it around the warrior's neck. He rubbed it gently with his thumb. Despite centuries of dust and debris and the unforgiving cycle of the elements, the stone had somehow maintained its luster. Bennett could only guess it was the result of the protection provided by layers of minerals that had formed around the body. And the dry mountain air and year-round cold temperatures were likely the reason for the well-preserved human tissue.

The longer Bennett looked at the stone, the more he wondered whether he was seeing a glow from within, emanating outward. After a moment, he chalked it up to reflection from his flashlight beam in the otherwise poorly lit space.

He scanned the full length of the body. He glanced over his shoulder at the altar, then back at the body.

"I think we've cleared away enough of the stone," he said. "I think we can move it."

Haluk looked up from the body and leveled is gaze at him, his eyes showing disbelief. "Move the body?" he said.

"Yeah. We can get a better look at it if we put it up on the altar. Eventually we're going to have to wrap up the remains anyway if we plan to take it down the mountain. It'll be easier to do if we're not kneeling on sharp rocks in this dark corner."

Haluk hesitated. He didn't answer. Bennett caught the apprehension look in his eyes.

"What is it?"

"We have found the stone. Is it wise to disturb the dead?"

"That sounds kind of superstitious. Weren't you just telling me a little while ago that stories about magic and mythology were meaningless in the modern age?"

"I was, yes," said Haluk. "Those things were easier to say when we both felt skeptical about the likelihood of finding Shi Zhu and the stone. But I am also concerned about time, and our safety. Would it not make more sense to just take the stone and keep moving?" He tilted his head toward the mouth of the cave. "It would be in our best interests to put as much distance as possible between us and our friends. Carrying these remains out of the cave and back down the mountain would just slow us down."

"The sun is completely down now," said Bennett.

"I understand," said Haluk. "But if we stay…"

"It's unlikely that they're moving right now, so they're not gaining any ground on us. We'll rest here for a couple hours, then head out at first light. We'll need some time to rig up some kind of stretcher that will enable us to take the remains back down the mountain without damaging them."

Haluk looked away for a moment. "I am not sure that I like the plan," he said, "but I cannot argue that I am very tired." He scanned the inside of the cave, as though weighing the situation.

"Very well," he said finally. "You are the boss, and I am the guide for hire. If you say we will stay, we will stay."

~ ~ ~

Less than a half hour later, Bennett and Haluk were arranging their sleeping bags about eight feet apart on the limited floor space of the cave, struggling to find something like a comfortable sleeping position amid the hard rock formations. The glow from a battery-powered lantern positioned between them threw strange shadows around the space.

Haluk tilted his chin toward the mouth of the cave and everything beyond it. "Our friends have followed us for nearly three days, and yet I am still not sure I understand how they know about any of this."

Bennett shook his head, doing his best to swallow his frustration. "Well, I suppose we can thank one man for that."

Haluk, down on one knee, stopped fussing with his gear and looked up at Bennett. His eyes formed a question.

"His name is Nathan Drake," said Bennett. "He's an archaeologist. By training and degree, anyway."

"A man like you."

Bennett's face twisted into a grimace. "He's nothing like me," he grunted. "His credentials may say he's an archaeologist, sure, but his reputation suggests something entirely different. His interest in history or science is secondary to his interest in his own wealth. He finds priceless artifacts and sells them to the highest bidder on the international black market. He's made enormous amounts of money by dealing with some of the most unsavory characters in the world. Nathan Drake is an unscrupulous son of a bitch. He's a mercenary and a pirate."

"What has set him on the trail of the stone?"

Bennett snorted and shook his head. "I suppose I did."

Haluk stopped suddenly and looked at him with a puzzled expression. "You?"

Bennett sighed. "A few weeks after bringing the scrolls back to the States, we arranged a couple small conferences on either side of the Atlantic—one in New York, the other in Zurich. The idea was to share the information with a very small, trusted group within the archeological community."

Bennett could feel the muscles of his jaw tightening at the mere memory of the events. "Barely an hour after the Zurich conference, I was approached in my hotel."

"By this Nathan Drake."

"Yes. He tried to appear friendly. He asked a lot of questions, as though we were just two colleagues sharing information with the common goal of expanding the canon of archaeological and historical knowledge."

"But you were not convinced."

"I didn't buy any of it, not for a second. His reputation preceded him. I kept my cards close to the vest."

Bennett picked up his canteen and unscrewed the cap. He took a short gulp of water and closed the container back up again. "And my worst suspicions were confirmed later that evening," he went on. "I had gone out of the hotel for dinner. When I came back, I discovered that many of the notes and records I had used in the presentation—including photographs and details about the map—were missing, and likely stolen."

"Stolen by Drake?"

"I had no proof at the time, and I still don't. But I don't need any. As I said, his reputation precedes him."

"And then," said Haluk, stumbling on the American figure of speech, "the cat had come out of the bag."

"Apparently so. Less than two weeks after the Zurich conference, the university was getting inquiries about the discovery. That was when I learned just how broad Drake's network of international connections really is. Word had gotten back to the Kremlin, and from there it was just a matter of time before a story about an extremely valuable stone in the mountains of China would get back to China itself."

"So it was suddenly important to move quickly to find the stone," said Haluk, "before someone else did."

Bennett nodded.

Haluk pondered the information silently for a moment. "So it is likely," he said, "that this Drake is among the men who are heading toward this same mountain and this same cave."

"I'd bet on it," said Bennett.

"But relations between the Soviets and China have been strained in recent years," said Haluk. "A man like Drake, whose influence is limited to the black market for ancient relics in Europe and the Soviet Union, would have a hard time assembling an expedition with members from two Communist superpowers."

Both men climbed into their sleeping bags and settled in.

"Hell, I don't know," said Bennett, reaching out and shutting off the lantern. "The layers of political espionage and intrigue between the Communist bloc and the West are a mystery to me. If this damn stone is as important as everyone seems to think it is, then I suspect money has changed hands. Lots of it, and probably the promise of even more once the stone is found. I'm just a scientist and a historian. I do my best to stay out of that kind of thing."

Haluk chuckled. "Your best does not appear to be very good, my friend. You said yourself that you are climbing mountains in a part of the world where an American—and his Turkish guide—could get into plenty of trouble."

"Which is why we're going to catch a couple hours sleep, gather up what we've found and get the hell out of here the minute we see light in the sky."

Haluk didn't answer. Within minutes, his breathing was deep and steady. But Bennett lay awake, staring into the darkness, hoping for an uneventful trip back down the mountain and into safer territory.

~ ~ ~

They missed the sunrise. It was a mistake that proved to be costly.

Maybe the climb had taken a heavier toll than they'd realized and they both slipped into a deeper and longer sleep than they'd planned. Maybe the thin mountain air disrupted their usual sleeping patterns. Whatever the case, Bennett awoke to sunlight pouring into the east-facing mouth of the cave.

He sat up and struggled to shake off the heavy veil of sleep. His first random thought was that the heavy cloud cover of the last several days had finally burned off.

And suddenly he was wide awake, and full of dread.

He checked his watch and swore under his breath. It was just a couple minutes before eight a.m., and the sun was well into the sky. The party that had been a half mile behind them the day before had likely been on the move since first light.

And then, as if in response to that last thought, he heard the sound that confirmed his worst fears.

Voices.

One speaking in Russian. Short and clipped. Efficient. Then another, also in Russian.

Bennett climbed out of the sleeping bag. He reached over to Haluk in his own sleeping bag and grabbed his arm. "Haluk!" he rasped, doing his best to keep his voice down but be forceful at the same time. "Wake up!"

The Turk jumped, and his eyes were suddenly wide. Bennett put a finger to his lips, then gestured toward the mouth of the cave.

Haluk glanced in the direction of the gesture as Bennett turned away and began rummaging furiously through his backpack in search of the revolver he had stashed in one of the compartments.

He was still rummaging when he heard Haluk say in a timid voice, "Mr. Jake."

Bennett looked up at Haluk, but Haluk's eyes were fixed on the entrance to the cave. Bennett turned to see a tall figure standing at the opening, backlit by the morning sun and throwing a long shadow across nearly a dozen feet of jagged stone floor inside the cave entrance.

"Whatever you are looking for, you can stop now," the figure said. "Take your hands out of the bag slowly and stand up straight. And put your hands where we all can see them."

By the time the voice had finished, there were three more figures in the cave entrance. Each of them held machine guns, and all of the weapons were pointed at Bennett and Haluk.

Bennett turned slightly and glanced at Haluk, whose eyes were wide and his hands already in the air as ordered. He figured the Turk probably had the right idea. He stopped rummaging, stood up straight and put up his hands.

The speaker took three steps into the cave. With less backlighting from the outside, it was clear now that the figure was holding a pistol, and the pistol was aimed across the space inside the cave at Bennett's chest.

"You are Mr. Bennett, yes? The KGB has told us about you." He was tall, thick framed, with an angular face. Whoever he was, he spoke precise English with a Russian accent.

Bennett didn't answer.

A fifth figure appeared from outside the cave and stepped in behind the Russian.

"Of course he is."

Bennett knew the voice immediately.

Nathan Drake.

"Hello, Jason," said the newcomer. "How wonderful to see a familiar face in such a remote location." He looked around the inside of the cave, trying to appear casual, as though he were admiring the new home of an old friend. But Bennett wasn't fooled. Drake was scanning the space for something in particular.

The Russian and the other three followed Drake deeper into the cave entrance. By now, Bennett could make out all of their faces. There was another Russian in addition to the one who'd come in first. Along with them were two Chinese.

"Drake," said Bennett, his voice dripping with sarcasm. "I can't imagine how you would have found me here."

Drake smiled back at him. He turned to the Russian with the pistol, then looked at the other three whose machine guns were trained on Bennett and Haluk. "Gentlemen, please," Drake said to all four of them. "There's no need to be uncivil."

The Russian with the pistol turned to the others and nodded. His expression showed reluctance. After a moment of hesitation, the guns lowered slowly.

Drake shook his head. "Where are my manners?" he said. "Some introductions are in order." He gestured at the Russian with the pistol. "This is Yuri Leonov. He's a…" Drake hesitated for a moment. "Well, he's been called many things. Mercenary. Pirate. But what's in a name? Let's just say he's a paid operative working for the Kremlin, and he has graciously agreed to lead this small but important expedition to this place—with some guidance from myself, of course."

Leonov locked eyes with Bennett, but neither man spoke.

Drake gestured toward the other Russian and the two Chinese. "That's Polichev, and the two charming fellows standing near him are Hong and Cho.

Leonov surveyed Haluk from head to toe, then spoke up. "And this silly little servant is…?"

"I am Haluk," said the Turk. His hands may have been in the air, but he held his head high and there was defiance in his eyes and his voice.

Drake regarded Haluk with a dismissive glance, then turned his full attention to Bennett. "So, Jason," he said, still feigning a conversational tone. "What brings you to these mountains, so far from your home in the U.S.?"

Bennett shrugged. "Oh, you know," he growled. "Just passing through."

Leonov smiled, but his face remained cold and hard. "You Americans," he said. "So witty and clever in the way you speak to authority. So it is in a country filled with cowboys and astronauts and… what do you call it…rock and roll."

Drake started to speak. "Alright, gentlemen, let's not—"

"Enough!" Leonov barked. "I will speak now." The Russian turned back to Bennett. "Drake has told me many things about you," he said. "Do not waste my time with your attempts at clever sarcasm. You were not just passing through. You came here looking for something very important, and we all know what it is. The question is, have you found it?"

Bennett shrugged. "I really don't know what you're—"

"You have come here, some seven-thousand miles away from the comfort of your universities and your museums and your libraries, in search of what the Chinese call the Stone of immortality. I have been told of the stories. I have been told of the map. There are some in my country, and even more in China, who actually believe that the stories and the legends are true."

"And you?"

Leonov laughed. "I do not know. Nor do I care. What I do know is that a high value has been placed upon the stone, and a large sum of money will be given to those who find it."

Hands still raised, Bennett glanced from one man to the next. He needed time to think, and he knew he might get it if he kept talking. "You know," he said finally, "for as awkward as this is, I have to say it's also heartwarming."

Leonov stared back at him. His eyes flared at Bennett's insolence, then slowly narrowed into an expression of suspicion. "What are you talking about?" he said finally.

"Two Russians and two Chinese, all together and working toward a common purpose. Haluk and I were just talking about this. We'd heard you were at odds, but it's nice to see everyone getting along so well."

Leonov glared back at Bennett, apparently trying to understand the point he was trying to make.

"Then again," Bennett went on, "I suppose that was always one thing you all could agree on—pointing as many missiles at the West as you could possibly manage."

"We did not come here to chat," said Leonov. "And we certainly did not come here to debate the ideology of the East and the West. That is what the Kremlin and your White House and the United Nations are for. You know why we are here. We have come to find the stone, and Drake is fairly certain—as am I—that you may have already done our work for us."

Bennett turned to Drake, who had been silent since Leonov's outburst. "So let me get this straight, Drake," he said. "You poached my research after the Zurich conference a couple months ago and immediately started shopping it around to that network of shady international contacts you call friends—which probably includes some foreign agents in countries that the United States doesn't exactly have warm and friendly relations with. Next thing you know, the Chinese want to talk to you. They see an opportunity to get their hands on something of great historical and cultural value. Hell, for all we know, some superstitious nutcase in Chairman Mao's inner circle actually believes this stone has all the power the legend claims it has. And I suspect a lot of money changed hands."

Drake shrugged. "I'm a businessman as much as a scientist."

"A lot of one and not much of the other," Bennett snarled. "But regardless of that, when the Chinese got wind of exactly where this thing might be, they got an idea."

He turned his attention to Leonov. "Nobody spends a lot of time in these mountains," he said to the Russian, "but this expedition of yours is an opportunity to survey the landscape and consider some strategic possibilities. From a military standpoint, this is prime real estate. Big mountain ranges like these are great places to hide weapons."

Bennett wasn't even sure if Polichev or the two Chinese operatives could even understand him, but he looked over at them and addressed the group as a whole. "Because that's the plan, isn't it, gentlemen? Get a hold of this artifact to make the chairman and maybe some members of his cultural ministry happy, and also lay the groundwork to set up a missile base up here. Maybe it was China's idea. Maybe it was Russia's idea…"

He paused for a moment to glance from face to face. "Given the demographic makeup of this merry little band, I'm thinking it was probably some kind of joint initiative. I know your two countries aren't as chummy as they were a few years ago, but hey, when the balance of global power is at stake, a good idea is a good idea, right?"

He turned back to Drake. "So in your efforts to exploit my research, you got yourself tangled up in a much bigger plan to point nuclear missiles at your own country," he said. "I'm no expert in foreign relations, but I'm pretty sure that's not going to go over well back home. This isn't just about one archaeologist stealing from another anymore. What you're doing here amounts to treason."

Maybe Drake was growing impatient, or maybe the suggestion of treason and what that could mean had unsettled him. Whatever the case, his friendly veneer had just about vanished. He took a couple steps closer to Bennett and looked at him with a burning gaze.

"You're standing in a cave that hasn't been visited by human beings for thirteen centuries," Drake said. His voice was low and dangerous, like the growl of a vicious dog. "You have guns pointed at your chest and no friends or allies for several thousand miles, save for this worthless lackey." He threw a contemptuous glance at Haluk, then looked back at Bennett. "I don't think you're in any position to tell me how much trouble I'm in right now."

He took a step backward and gestured toward the sunlight coming through the mouth of the cave. "The sky is clear for the first time in days," he said, pasting a smile on his face and resuming some of his earlier convivial tone. "It's a beautiful day for traveling in the outdoors. And none of us has time for this chatter, anyway. So you will hand over the stone if you have it—or tell us where in this godforsaken mountain we can find it—and then we will be on our way."

Bennett snorted. "Who are you kidding? I know how this gets played. I tell you where the stone is, you take it and then you kill us, right?"

Drake smiled and shrugged. "I said we would be on our way. I never said anything about any details we would take care of before we left."

Bennett's mind raced. The stone was the bargaining chip, the only one he and Haluk had to play with. As long as they knew where it was and Drake and the others didn't, they'd stay alive. If they gave it up, they'd be dead in a matter of minutes.

"I don't know where it is," he said. "There are hundreds of caves in these mountains. I thought we'd found the right one but I was mistaken."

Leonov stepped forward. "You are lying!" he grunted. "We followed the same map that you followed, and we came to the same place. How could we both be wrong?"

"I'm telling you the truth," said Bennett. He turned and pointed to their sleeping bags and other gear on the cave floor. "Look, we spent the night here. If we'd found the stone here last night, why would we stick around and wait for you to show up? Hell, that's the archaeological find of the century. If we'd found that thing in here, we'd have been gone within an hour."

Leonov looked back at him without a word, weighing the logic. After what seemed like almost thirty seconds, he turned to Hong and grunted a command in Chinese.

Hong stepped forward without hesitation and grabbed Haluk by the arm. The Turk struggled to wrench himself away, but Hong was at least five inches taller than Haluk and at least fifty pounds heavier.

Leonov issued another command, and Hong produced a hunting knife from some hidden sheath on his belt. He held the edge of the knife to Haluk's neck and applied just enough pressure to produce a small trickle of blood.

Bennett quickly weighed whatever options he might have left. In the end there were none. He wouldn't stand by and watch his guide—his friend—undergo unspeakable horrors over a hunk of jade, however valuable it might be.

"Alright!" he said. "Let him go. I'll tell you where it is."

And as he said the words, the morning sun rose just high enough in the east to pour a ray of light into the opening in the ceiling of the cave.

~ ~ ~

For Bennett, the next horrifying moments seemed to unfold in slow motion.

First came the long shadow that rose up behind him, dimming the light in the cave just seconds after the sunlight began streaming into the open space above.

But there was still enough light for Bennett to see the expression of smug self-assurance melt away from Drake's face as his gaze drifted upward to a place somewhere above and behind Bennett. Drake's eyes went wide and his mouth dropped open at the sight of something horrific that Bennett couldn't immediately see.

Bennett spun just in time to see Hong unwrap his arm from around Haluk's neck. The Chinese operative looked upward and let out a guttural noise that was equal parts surprise, disbelief and terror.

Bennett kept turning in the direction of Hong's terrified gaze and stumbled backward at the sight of what had risen up behind him.

The mummified body, no longer lifeless and wrapped in a decaying animal pelt, stood tall on the altar just beneath the aperture in the cave ceiling. His menacing form, covered with gray, leathery skin and a few persistent fragments of the animal hide, had somehow grown to a stature much taller and larger than any seventh-century Chinese warrior could have stood—certainly much more powerful than the fragile and lifeless thing Bennett and Haluk had found half-buried in the rock.

The thing stood still for a moment, its shoulders hunched and its legs spread apart—as though it were ready to engage in battle. It turned its head slowly from side to side, surveying the room and everyone in it, making a sound that might have been breathing or might have been a low and persistent growl.

It had no eyes to speak of. Instead, two glowing red orbs burned in its skull with an unholy flame. As Bennett struggled to keep looking at the thing, the muscles of its face tightened against its jaw and pulled away from its teeth to create a horrific grimace.

My God, thought Bennett. *It's true. It's all true.*

This horrific, man-like thing—born of another age yet profoundly menacing in the here and now—was Shi Zhu, the great warrior and protector of the ancient temple of Khotan, brought back to the world of the living thirteen centuries after his time by the ancient Stone of Immortality.

And if all of this weren't fearsome enough, the thing was fully armed for battle—sword in the right hand and shield strapped to the left forearm. It had slept for centuries in this cold and desolate place, and yet in the moments since the light had awakened it by triggering the power of the stone, it had instantly retrieved its weapons and re-armed itself after more than a thousand years—as though mere moments had passed.

The thing had to be nearly eight feet tall, by Bennett's best guess. Did the stone, with all of its power to reanimate, also enhance size and strength? There was no way for Bennett to know, and right now, it was the least of his concerns.

Hong, who'd been restraining Haluk just moments earlier, was the first to regain enough composure to sheath his knife and unleash a rapid-fire burst from his machine gun. This quickly proved to be a bad idea.

The thing roared. It was a hellish sound made even more terrifying by the echo of the cave and its various side corridors. It leaped off the altar directly into Hong's line of fire.

Hong responded with several more bursts of gunfire at the oncoming beast, each more erratic than the last as the tremor of fear in his hands grew more severe with the thing's unchecked advance. The barrage of slugs slammed into Shi Zhu's upper body, and he jerked slightly as fragments of gray flesh were torn away from his torso.

But the giant kept coming. It took a step forward and reached a long sinewy arm toward Hong. The gunman tried to back away, but he stumbled on some uneven rock formations and fell backward. Before Hong could regain his footing, Shi Zhu reached down and grabbed the gun from Hong's right hand and flung it across the cave where it disappeared into a dark corner. The giant pointed his sword directly at Hong's neck. It hesitated for a moment, then drove the blade deep into his throat.

The thrust resulted in a horrifying a combination of rasping and gurgling, followed by a wave of crimson that spilled across Hong's chest and onto the rock floor underneath him. Within seconds, Hong was still and lifeless, his head turned at a ghastly angle from the lower part of his neck and nearly severed from his shoulders.

Leonov immediately dispensed with his pistol and opened fire on the giant with his machine gun. Polichev and Cho raised their weapons and joined the rapid-fire chorus. Drake, standing apart from the other three, had drawn a pistol of his own and joined the other three in the full assault. The combined barrage of gunfire filled the cave with a prolonged and deafening roar.

On its surface, the response might have seemed decisive and confident, but the looks in the three men's eyes told the tale. The barrage of bullets was partly a calculated defensive maneuver and partly a primal response to the unspeakable terror that was just beginning to unfold.

Bennett moved without thinking. In a single instinctive maneuver, he leaped toward Haluk and tackled him into a corner that was mostly out of the line of fire but far from completely safe.

The three mercenaries were no longer paying any attention to Bennett and Haluk. Fending off the enormous thing that had risen up before them and viciously killed one of their own was now their sole concern. The thing jerked and twitched at the fusillade of high-caliber slugs fired at close range. But other than bits of hide tearing away from its frame, the thing appeared to experience no pain. Nor did it fall.

Instead, it opened its maw and issued another unearthly roar that merged with the machine-gun fire. Bennett and Haluk ducked reflexively from the sound, squeezing their eyes shut and pressing their hands to their ears.

The thing advanced directly into the oncoming assault. In a lightning-fast motion, it raised its shield and brought it down with a deadly force. The sweeping blow tore the machine guns out of the hands of Polichev and Cho and crushed the weapons against the cave floor, where they shattered like matchsticks.

Cho was immediately howling at the sudden destruction of his weapon. At first Bennett thought it was the sound of anger or defiance, but he quickly realized that it was something else. It was a wail of pain.

Doing his best to stay hidden behind a vertical rock formation, Bennett glanced over his shoulder at the two piles of mangled steel and shattered wood that had been a pair of deadly weapons just seconds earlier. Something amid the pieces of broken firearms looked wrong, even amid the madness that had erupted in the small space of the cave. Something stained with red, about two feet long and glistening in the incoming sunlight, had fallen to the ground with the rest of the machine gun fragments.

Bennett looked back at Cho, hunched and screaming and holding his right arm with his left hand. The gunman turned slightly and stumbled to his knees, and suddenly Bennett understood.

The glistening thing on the ground was Cho's right forearm. The giant had hacked it off just above the elbow when he brought the shield down on the machine guns. Cho slumped to the ground and landed on his side, his left hand still holding what was left of his right arm in an attempt to contain the severe hemorrhaging from the mangled stump of a limb. But Bennett knew the effort was in vain. Cho would bleed out in a few more seconds.

Polichev, the Russian gunman, made no effort to help his comrade. Instead he stumbled backward, quickly losing his footing on the uneven cave floor. The giant stalked him, taking broad steps that hammered against the stone floor and quickly closed the distance between himself and his prey. The sight of the thing coming toward him forced an involuntary moan of terror from some deep and craven place within Polichev.

The Russian turned its back and tried to crawl across and around the uneven rock floor on all fours, but the giant came up behind him and clamped his enormous left hand on the Russian's shoulder. He raised his sword in his right hand and brought it down hard on Polichev's opposite shoulder.

Bennett heard the soft sound of tearing flesh, the crack of a collarbone, the painful scream of the damned as Polichev's shoulder was nearly torn away from the rest of his torso. The giant brought the blade back up and, with his left hand still on the Russian's left shoulder, lifted the gunman off the ground and hurled him like a grain sack across the interior of the cave. Polichev slammed headfirst against an unforgiving rock wall and left a smear of blood on the uneven surface as he slid to the floor. Bennett took one look at the crumpled body as it came to rest and knew immediately the Russian was dead.

Leonov had positioned himself behind a rock formation and laid low, watching in horror as the giant had mangled and destroyed his comrades one by one. Hands shaking, he steadied his machine gun against a horizontal ledge of rock and began firing. The gun erupted in a few short bursts, but as with the other offensives, his bullets accomplished nothing more than tearing a few random bits of leathery flesh from the beast's towering frame.

If anything, the gunfire had neutralized Leonov's minimal advantage by signaling his position to the beast. The thing turned in the direction of the oncoming barrage. Its face twitched, as though it were momentarily sniffing the air, and it began its advance—directly into the staccato hail of bullets.

With each step the giant took, the gunfire became more continuous. Bennett could almost hear Leonov's panic in the seemingly endless drone of slugs that crossed the inside of the cave and slammed into the Shi Zhu's ominous frame without stopping it.

And then the bullets stopped altogether. Bennett heard a *click-click-click,* punctuated by a gasp and a curse. The overheated gun had obviously jammed, leaving Leonov suddenly and hopelessly defenseless.

Moving with a speed that defied his enormous size and weight, the giant sidestepped the gunman's small rock barricade and grabbed the machine gun with its right claw. The thing raised its arm and slammed the weapon against the rocks, where it shattered into several pieces that went skittering in all directions.

Leonov stumbled backward and found himself trapped in the convergence of two vertical rock formations butting against each other. Like Polichev, Leonov was now backed into a corner with no option for escape.

Leonov screamed, but the sound was cut off as the beast reached out swiftly and grabbed him by the throat. Leonov kicked and jerked and clawed at the fist at his neck as the thing held him at arm's length and raised him above its head, a good ten feet into the air. In a single, swift thrust, the thing dashed Leonov against an outcropping of stalagmites jutting up from the floor.

Bennett heard an enormous burst of air erupt from Leonov as he landed on his back on the cave floor. The Russian's eyes were wide, his arms and legs flailed helplessly, and his face had gone white with pain and shock. Bennett looked at the man's chest and puzzled for a moment at the odd protrusion from inside his shirt.

The beast raised the same arm it had used to hurl Leonov to the ground and clenched a fist. With lightning speed and blinding force, it brought the fist down onto Leonov's chest. Bennett heard the sharp crack of ribs as the force of the blow drove the Russian's body further down onto the rocks and brought him to a ghastly finish.

Leonov died instantly, his lifeless eyes staring upward in a frozen gaze of horror and his torso impaled by two stalagmites that had driven into his back and emerged through his chest.

Bennett looked away reflexively, his mind barely able to grasp the horrifying site.

That left Drake, wide-eyed and terrified, holding an empty pistol in a hand trembling beyond control.

The beast stood still for a moment, scanning the space within the cave with its glowing eyes. Drake had curled himself into a dark corner, apparently hoping to find cover in the shadows, but his breath came shallow and fast, occasionally punctuated by a whimper that he couldn't seem to control.

After a moment, the beast turned slowly in the direction of the tiny, frightened sounds emerging from the shadows and dropped the sword and shield. It started to move, following the pathetic sounds emerging from the shadows. After only two steps, it was clear to Bennett that the thing had found Drake. And it was clear that Drake knew it. With each step the beast took, the whimpering from the shadows grew more urgent.

"Oh God...Oh God..." Drake's quivering voice was the bleat of a helpless lamb in the den of a ravenous lion.

The giant moved closer to Drake's hiding place in the shadows, getting a better sense of its bearings with each step. And with each step, the terror in Drake's voice inched closer to hysteria.

"Oh God, no!" he wailed. "Bennett! Bennett, please! *Bennett! Help me!*"

He was shrieking now as the beast took larger and more decisive strides in his direction.

Bennett almost called to Drake, thinking he might somehow help him find a way out of his doomed corner. But his instinct for self-preservation silenced him. For all he knew, any sound he made could turn the beast in his direction and seal his own fate.

Drake's terror-stricken sounds quickly devolved into ghastly gibberish—an unholy mix of shrieking, gasping, pleading, all of it underscored by the desperate sound of arms and legs scrambling against unforgiving rock for some way out of the darkness he'd backed himself into.

And then the thing was upon him.

A gnarled hand snaked around Drake's neck with a grip so fierce that Bennett thought Drake's upper vertebrae might snap. Drake responded by kicking instinctively with his right leg in a desperate attempt to keep the thing at bay.

The thing grabbed the jerking limb with its free hand and made a fierce wrenching motion. The result was unmistakable. The odd angle at which Drake's leg now jutted away from his lower torso body could only mean a severe dislocation.

Painful though it must have been, Drake was unable to cry out. Though his eyes and mouth were both agape, the vise grip around his neck had reduced his voice to a gurgling, rasping noise.

If the beast was even aware of Bennett or Haluk, it gave no sign of it. Its sole focus was this last of the violent intruders—the remaining attacker whose elimination was his sworn duty. It dragged Drake like a twitching rag doll toward the mouth of the cave, toward the sunlight and the mountains beyond, toward the sweeping vista of a homeland it hadn't seen in more than thirteen hundred years.

His leg damaged and askew, Drake could gain no footing on the uneven stone floor as the thing yanked him toward the light from beyond the entrance to the cave. He flailed with both arms, but the pain in his leg—combined with a constricted airway and a crippling terror—had sapped his strength and rendered him all but helpless.

And then they were outside. Bennett and Haluk dared to step just a few inches outside their hiding place to see through the doorway to the cave. Without a sound, the two men watched the grisly dance continue under the open sky and against the panoramic mountain vista.

Haluk stood slightly behind Bennett, peering around his shoulder. "Mr. Jake..." he began in an urgent whisper.

Without taking his eyes off the brutal scene unfolding beyond the cave door, Bennett put a hand up to quiet his guide. He shook his head slowly. "There's..." he began in a similar whisper. "There's nothing we can do for him."

The thing continued to drag Drake away from the cave. After a few steps, it was clear where it was headed.

It was taking Drake to the edge of the cliff at the opposite edge of the path.

And it was apparent, even from where Bennett was standing in the cave, that Drake knew it too. He suddenly began thrashing and flailing against the monster's iron grip with renewed energy. He managed to push enough air through his constricted throat to release a pinched and terror-stricken sound that turned Bennett's stomach. But this last-ditch, spastic effort was not nearly enough to fend off the rage-driven beast's inhuman strength.

After a few more long strides, Shi Zhu reached the edge of the path and the cliff just beyond it. Drake, unable to support himself on his damaged leg, struggled to anchor himself on one foot and at the same time push himself away from the beast and away from the yawning chasm just a few inches from where the thing had dragged him.

Slowly, silently, Bennett and Haluk followed the thing out of the cave and into the sunlight and cutting wind, taking care to keep at least thirty or forty feet between themselves and the beast and stay out of its direct line of sight. The thing was clearly preoccupied with Drake. If it noticed them at all, it gave no indication.

The thing held Drake around the neck and dragged him the last few inches to the edge of the cliff. Drake fought back, grasping and clawing convulsively at the gnarled fingers curled around his neck and the wiry forearm at the other end of the hand.

It was effort wasted. Shi Zhu dwarfed him in size and strength. Drake was no more than a crippled bird flailing hopelessly in the grip of a much larger and more powerful predatory beast.

And then it dragged him over the side, and Drake screamed anew as his damaged leg scraped across the jagged edge of rock and ice. With its hand still wrapped around Drake's neck, the thing knelt at the very edge of the cliff and stared through angry, glowing eyes at the horrified face that was now looking up and back at him and gibbering for mercy.

Bennett and Haluk took a few steps across the path, just close enough to see Drake's face over the side of the cliff. The ghastly mix of pain and mind-bending terror on the man's face nearly turned

Bennett's stomach.

Haluk whispered, "My God..." His voice instantly choked off. He could find no other words.

Drake flailed and clawed at the beast, scraping a few remaining fragments of animal pelt and even loose bits of flesh off the thing's arm. But the force around his neck was powerful and unrelenting.

In a last desperate grasp, he reached up and grabbed hold of the leather thong that held the stone around Shi Zhu's neck. The beast reached up to its own neck with a free hand and tried to yank the leather strap out of Drake's tenuous grip, but Drake held on.

In a final yank between Drake and the unholy beast, the leather thong snapped, and what had been a loop was now two feet of leather with a desperate hand grasping either end. The sudden jerk resulting from the break threw both of them off balance. Drake seized the opportunity as his last hope for survival and held on to his end of the broken strip like a drowning soul at the end of a tattered lifeline.

To the limited extent to which Bennett could recognize an expression on the giant's ghoulish features, Shi Zhu seemed suddenly surprised that the life-giving stone—the sacred thing he had been sworn for centuries to protect—could have come away from his neck so easily and now hang suspended in such a precarious space over the edge of the cliff. Seemingly confused, the beast loosened its grip on Drake's neck.

Drake countered by reaching up with his free hand—the one not clutching the leather strap—and grabbing at the thing's shoulder. He was struggling for any opportunity to regain some small advantage that might somehow get him back onto the top of the cliff.

But the giant shrugged away and pushed back at him, and whatever grip Drake had gained was just as quickly lost. Drake gasped for air, obviously fighting against physical pain and the sheer terror of yawning empty space underneath his dangling feet.

He reached again in a final frantic attempt, waving his hand, searching for something—anything to hold onto. His hand found the stone itself, still bound to the leather strap by a small ring of iron.

Clearly angered by Drake's persistence, the beast shrugged again and reached down, attempting to wrench Drake's hand away from the stone.

Bennett heard a soft twisting sound, followed by a snap.

The thong had severed somewhere near the mid-point, the pliant leather stretched to its limits after suspending the full weight of Drake's struggling form over the edge of the cliff.

Drake vanished into the abyss. Bennett was too far from the edge of the cliff to fathom the full length of the fall. He could only guess the distance from the sound of Drake's scream, which never really ended so much as faded into what seemed like eternity.

The giant looked down at the broken fragment of leather in its hand. The beast's shoulders sagged. For all of its size and strength and savagery, it looked somehow defeated, suddenly diminished. Almost tragic.

The stone had fallen into the abyss with Drake, and with it had gone the mysterious life force that had reanimated the warrior once known as Shi Zhu.

The thing rose to its feet, but never quite stood erect. It never threw its shoulders back or raised its eyes to the bright expanse of clear sky. Instead, it kept its face toward the ground.

"Mr. Jake," Haluk whispered. "We must hide. If he turns to see us—"

Bennett put a hand up. "Wait," he said, his voice not much more than a whisper. "I don't think he—"

Before he could finish, Shi Zhu turned slowly to face them. Haluk uttered a small gasp, but Bennett raised a hand again to quiet him. He thought he noticed something about the beast's skin—a subtle change in texture and color, perhaps—but he wasn't sure if the sunlight may have been playing tricks on his eyes after days of heavy cloud cover.

Hands empty of weapons, frame no longer poised for battle, the beast looked at Bennett and Haluk for a long moment through the ominous fiery orbs deep in its skull. As it stood looking at them, Bennett was now certain that its skin was changing, darkening, withering in the sunlight.

Bennett almost tried to speak, but he knew that if this being understood any language at all in this strange reanimated state of half-life and half-death, twentieth century English would mean nothing to him.

As Bennett weighed this logic, Shi Zhu did something startling.

He opened his mouth and spoke.

"*Shítou,*" he said. His voice was a raspy whisper that Bennett could barely hear amid the wind slicing through the mountains.

"I...I'm sorry...I don't..."

"*Shítou.*"

"Shítou," said Bennett, searching his mind for a moment. It's Chinese. He's saying 'stone.'"

"Are you going to tell him?" said Haluk. "Because I do not want to be the one to tell him."

The beast looked sad. What's more, Bennett could now clearly see bits of flesh flaking away from Shi Zhu's limbs and torso and drifting away in the wind. "I think he already knows."

Bennett looked directly into the glowing orbs. Their intensity seemed diminished in the aftermath of the carnage. "Shítou," he said again addressing the giant. "The stone. I'm sorry."

"*Shítou,*" said the beast.

"You're fate was a hard one," said Bennett, fairly certain that the thing didn't understand.

The warrior's right hand dried up and flaked away from his wrist and disappeared into the wind. A few seconds later, a portion of his forearm went with it.

For all of the giant's ferocity just minutes before, Bennett was struck by a wave of sympathy and regret. This forsaken creature, this damned soul, had once been a noble warrior committed to protecting a hallowed place of peace and a cherished way of life. Thirteen hundred years later, a convergence of mystical power and cruel fate had awakened him from a long slumber—but only for a brief moment before sending him to oblivion.

Haluk must have felt it too. He took a few steps away from Bennett and toward Shi Zhu as the giant's right leg buckled and then gave out from under him. "Mr. Jake," said Haluk as the warrior fell to one knee. The Turk's voice was filled with the same sense of regret that had struck Bennett. "He…he is wasting away. Surely there must be some way to…"

Shi Zhu was on both knees now, and both legs were quickly crumbling to dust and drifting off in the wind.

Bennett reached out and grabbed Haluk's arm gently, "No," he said. "There's nothing we can do. His time in this world is finally finished. He protected the stone from the invaders. Unfortunately the stone gave him a gift he couldn't hold onto for long."

The giant looked back at Bennett and Haluk one last time. With no other words, with no further sound, the last vestiges of flesh and bone that made up his head and torso dissolved into a swirl of dust that merged with the icy wind and took to the air toward other parts of the vast mountain range.

Shi Zhu was no more. And the Stone of Immortality, the closest thing to proof that he had ever existed at all, was now interred somewhere in the infinite layers of snow and ice and rock of the Kunlun.

Bennett and Haluk stood on the path and stared out over the cliff at the sea of peaks and valleys that stretched for nearly two-thousand miles. Neither could think of much to say.

Their journey home would be a long one.

SACRIFICES

by Nancy Hansen

S he was dragged before the warlord of the opposing tribe, still
splattered with the blood of her enemies. She glared at him de-
fiantly as she was forced to kneel. He spoke, and though she could
not understand what he said, the meaning was obvious.

The leader stepped forward and lifted her chin. She had fine features with dark eyes and hair, but the scowl she gave him was pure
malevolence. He laughed. "She is strong-willed and bold, but I will
tame her. I plan to keep this one as a concubine. She will bear me
many fine warrior sons."

Baring her teeth like an animal, she launched a vicious kick into
his groin and then spat in his face. She would submit to no man. His
fist knocked her head sideways and she slumped in the guards' arms

"Stake her out and lash her ten times for every man she has killed
today," the warlord said with a snarl. "Then we shall see how brave
she is."

She knew those of her people who were already in captivity
would be watching how she conducted herself under torture, so she
controlled her response. As the first strokes fell, she clamped her
lips shut to keep from crying out. The horse whip bit in again and
again, raising welts that opened into lacerations that bled freely.

The pain was almost unendurable. She chanted a litany to the gods, willing strength to her people to endure, and promising to guard them always.

They had to change men because the arm of the one wielding the whip grew tired. Eventually she did lose consciousness and the beating stopped.

"What do we do with her now?" the men who had watched asked.

"A woman who does not submit to a man is useless. Bury her and we move on."

A rough grave was dug by conquered villagers from the area. She was thrown in, unconscious but still alive. Her eyes flew open and she tried to claw her way out as dirt and rocks rained down. The weight kept her pinned against the ice beneath, but she screamed invectives until she coughed and choked as frozen bits of grit filled her mouth. Soon there was no light, no air. Her eyes rolled back as her lungs collapsed, and her body convulsed in death.

~ ~ ~

The team leader met her at the airport in Barnaul.

"Dr. Ramos, I am Lyov Polzin. I am very glad to have you join us. How was your flight?"

"Long and bumpy," the short, dark haired woman with the big round glasses quipped. She stretched cramped muscles and yawned. The tall man with the narrow face extended a hand and she quickly shook it while a porter took her single bag and carefully placed it in the waiting vehicle—an aging UAZ-469 in rust-bubbled battleship green. Dr. Marcela Ramos had been to many dig sites over her fourteen years as professor of anthropological archaeology at Renton University in Washington State, and she had learned to carry only what she needed. "What do we have going on here, Mr. Polzin?"

"Call me Lyov, please." He tilted his head toward a group of men standing by. "I can explain more over dinner at the hotel," he said in a low voice. "But we have found a burial site with a frozen mummy, and it appears to be incredibly intact." His pale blue eyes sparkled when she rounded her lips into a little 'O' shape.

"Very interesting," Marcela said in a noncommittal tone as she clambered up into the vehicle's front passenger side. She had to slam the dented door twice to get it to stay shut. A minister of the local government got in behind her, and she stifled a groan. You would think they'd be past this Cold War nonsense by now.

The drive out to the hosting area was about three hours long. That and an early dinner killed most of the afternoon. They did not get to talk much, as their taciturn 'guide,' Mr. Serpionov, was always hovering nearby. "We will lose him in the morning once we are headed to the Altai," Polzin reassured Marcela before they went to their rooms.

The wakeup summons came pre-dawn, but anyone who has worked in the field expects that. A light breakfast and they were on the road, headed generally east. At the first rest stop of the morning their guide parted with them after going over a tediously long sheet of 'dos and don'ts.' Some bottled water and a quick bite and they were off again, bumping cross-country. Talking was difficult because of the rough ride, but along the way, Polzin filled her in as they bounced around on and off dirt roads and splashed through streams and rivers. Thankfully his English was good, if a bit accented.

"We were informed of a spring thaw sinkhole in an area that is slated for development of a proposed gas pipeline. At first they thought it was a collapsed pingo, since the area was once all permafrost. Someone from the government's geological department came out and found that indeed a hollowed spot had caved in on itself, and that there was a shallow grave site within. That turned out to be a skeletonized burial, but nothing spectacularly exciting. Likely just local herders. They would have removed the contents to a museum, filled it in, and continued on, but there was local outcry against it. That is how my people got called in. When our team came out to investigate, we realized there was a lower level to this grave that contained another burial that is much older. That is where the mummy lies."

"You said it was well preserved?" she queried, watching the countryside go by. Taiga forests close to the mountains receded before flatter land with some scrub, which gave way to grassy steppes as they bounced along dirt roads.

"Incredibly so! The mummy was in the permafrost, and lies in what has become an ice chamber. From what we can see she is naked and recognizably female. There are tattoos on her skin, long hair and fingernails. It's not a ritual burial because there are no textiles, personal ornamentation or artifacts, nor any food laid out. I thought you would want to see it in situ because she is such a perfect specimen. We can learn so much from her."

"I'm surprised you waited for me," Marcela admitted. "It sounds like an incredible find."

"Oh, it is," Polzin assured her. "However, there have been some problems..."

Marcela sighed. There were always problems. "The government?" she guessed.

"No. The locals. We have a mixed group of activist Russians backed by outside preservation groups and indigenous herders. There have been protests, but I am more concerned about some issues with sabotage."

"Really?" she said, peering over at him. "Grave robbers?"

"No, there is nothing to take but the body itself, and that is still frozen in a block of ice. However, we have had multiple equipment failures, unexplained illnesses, and wildlife rampaging through the camp. Several of our volunteers became unnerved and have left after one man was mauled at night by something large with claws and teeth. We assume it was a bear. We had to have him airlifted by a helicopter so his wounds could be properly treated."

"That does sound rather coincidental," she said evenly, but Marcela was uneasy, and she stroked the gold cross necklace she always wore. She began to see why they had called her in. She had long studied the supernatural belief systems and death rites of indigenous people, and had a great respect for the strength of their commitment to the tenets of their faith. Often in these isolated areas, those core beliefs were carried down through hundreds if not thousands of years. While such field calamities were not unheard of, they tended to happen regularly around controversial digs. Her more skeptical peers shrugged it off as happenstance or possibly local vandalism. Marcela was not always comfortable with a purely scientific viewpoint.

Polzin's voice broke into her musing as he muscled the vehicle around a tight turn.

"The locals are particularly attached to their cultural traditions. They do not want the gravesites of what they believe are their ancestors disturbed. Yet in spite of their ongoing disapproval, the gas pipeline is still going through."

"That's sad. Is it necessary to disturb this sacred ground?"

He sighed impatiently. "Where is the ground not sacred to someone? Yes, it must go through here, because it is the only pass to China. The revenue of the pipeline will provide a better standard of living for all. Natural gas is my country's most salable commodity, and China is a dependable customer. These herders do not understand that. They were already upset that there is talk of building a highway, because so many visitors have come on pilgrimages to the mountains. Wealthy Russians and those from other countries want to experience rural life and get close to native roots, and will gladly pay for the privilege, boosting the local economy.

She looked at him strangely while bracing herself for yet another bumpy turn. "What do you think I can accomplish here? I'm a stranger, and no one outside the academic branch knows me well. This find should go to one of your museums."

"Ah, but there is an advantage in having a foreign authority step in," he said with a sly smile. "You are a well-respected lecturer from America whose face is more recognizable than you believe. People in powerful positions have seen you on the international news channels, and they will be awed that such a remote find brought you to this part of the world. As scientists, we both understand the state of permafrost melting up here that exposed the site. If we want to know more about this woman, we will have to remove her remains. As for the locals, well, even they have some understanding of your type of expertise. They know the government will prevail and the gas pipeline will eventually be installed, and just as likely, that highway will become a reality. You have spoken often about preserving the heritage of the past, so that whatever you say about the deteriorating climate should convince them to let us remove the mummy from the site. In an American museum, you have the funds and the technology to see that it will be properly handled and tested. Later perhaps it can come back."

Polzin's confident tone suggested that this plan had already been approved by those above him, even if it flew in the face of local wishes. Obviously the government was paying Polzin and his team to handle the public outcry, so they had agreed to let him bring in an American "expert" to tell everyone what should be done. Marcela did not like being involved with such schemes, but she had been in similar situations before. The most important part was cataloging and safeguarding these very fragile bits of history.

"Let me see what you have, and we'll proceed from there," she told him. She wasn't going to promise anything until she'd verified that it was worth the effort it would take to remove the remains intact. Marcela Ramos was less than happy about having her name connected to yet another controversial dig, though they did make for successful book tours and interesting lecture material.

~ ~ ~

It was an incredible find. She was not sorry she had come.

The steppe area where the dig was located was a high valley in the mountains. Cold and windswept from the surrounding slopes, even daytime temperatures required warm layers of clothing. Marcela shivered as she climbed down into the pit. The team had erected a sort of shelter over the grave site, but even so, temperatures would warm up as the day went on, and she feared for the integrity of the mummy.

"There is no prominent kurgan height, judging from the countryside around it," Marcela scribbled in her notebook as she sat on scaffolding and surveyed the ice below via portable lighting. *"Soil stratifica-*

tion indicates that the permafrost here was quite thick at interment, and that seems to have kept the remains from decomposing. It has gradually receded over time.

"A second body from another era was buried atop this one. We believe that breach let in the water that displaced much of the dirt and rocks covering her, creating the ice chamber that further preserved her remains. Much of the ice is gone now, the remainder is mostly in and around the body itself.

"No apparent grave goods. Lack of ritual suggests she was either disgraced or interred by another tribe. What I can see of the mummy appears contorted, her arms up over her face protectively, so she may have been buried well after rigor mortis or a fatal seizure. The amazing thing is the level of preservation. From what we see through the ice, she is nearly intact. We need to move her remains ASAP, and get her back to a lab that can handle frozen finds before she deteriorates any further." She underscored that last sentence twice.

Now she could understand Polzin's insistence that she come view it herself. The mummy would have to be transported frozen, and he likely did not have the contacts for that. Marcela did, and her mind was already racing with the possibilities. This would be such a coup for her university's museum.

"Whatever you do," she told the archaeologists in charge of the dig, "don't try and thaw her out. Get the entire burial loose in a single block of ice, and then we'll have to wrap it thickly. I'll see about getting some sort of refrigerated truck in here to take her to the airport. We want to keep her frozen until we can get her back to the U.S., where we can put her in climate control and gradually thaw down to the level of the body. This is just too well-preserved a specimen to handle carelessly."

Marcela wasn't the leader of the dig, but the people around her responded eagerly to someone willing to take charge. Certainly Polzin didn't mind, for he was all smiles. Marcela, however, wasn't smiling. She had not slept well the night before, waking several times from vivid dreams of potential calamities. It was likely just nerves. Then in the wee hours before dawn there had been some sort of mild earthquake. It had done little damage, other than knocking down the makeshift shelter over the dig when some of the excavated soil and rocks slumped back in. All had to be laboriously removed before she could enter to do her site inventory.

Marcela was just climbing back out via a freestanding ladder when a rock the size of her head somehow loosened and came bounding down at her. She let out a frightened yelp, and ducked sideways, clinging by one hand and a leg as it began to pull away from the wall. Fortunately someone above pulled the ladder back in place just in time to keep her from falling helplessly into the pit.

She climbed up the rest of the way on shaking limbs, unnerved but also furious for the carelessness of whomever left heavy material like that so close by. Even with a hard hat on, she could have been seriously injured if not killed outright had it caught her.

It was Polzin who had caught the ladder, and he reached down to help her up. "You are not injured, I hope?" he inquired with honest concern.

"I'm fine," she said, accepting his hand. "But your people must be more cautious. Someone could have been badly hurt."

"It will not happen again," he promised her. He saw her safely to the tent they had set up as an on-site commissary and medic station, and then went back and harangued his entire crew in short bursts of angry Russian.

Of course no one took responsibility for the situation. Most of them had vacated the area to let the renowned American scientist work in peace while they sifted soil with screens and sorted through the day's finds. It was chalked up to another freak incident. With the afternoon winding down, Polzin and Marcela broke off work so they could discuss the situation.

Marcela had noted the somber vigil kept by a small crowd just outside the cordoned area of the dig. Local people being held back by guards cried out angrily, and she felt rather guilty. Part of their heritage was going to be carried off by strangers, and it was hard to understand why this was for the best. Their voices were strident; weathered faces lined with concern.

"What are they saying, Lyov?" Marcela asked over a dinner of canned soup, crackers, and tea. She tilted her head, indicating the protesters still outside the impromptu fence.

"It is nothing important," he said dismissively, waving his hand like he was shooing flies.

"Well it must be to them, or they wouldn't still be here," she said with an edge to her voice. Polzin's indifferent attitude toward these native Altai residents, who considered themselves the descendants of the mummified woman in the dig site, rankled her. As an anthropologist, she had a great respect for cultures that remained remote enough to have not yet been completely absorbed by modern society and all its trappings, because there were so few left. "You did want me to speak to them, didn't you?"

He sighed and set down his enameled metal cup on the rickety folding camp table. "At some point, yes, Marcela. But I was more concerned that you address groups like the World Wildlife Fund and UNESCO, because they have more of what you Americans would call 'clout.' These people want to hold back progress for the entire country based on a few old gravesites." There was so much disdain in his voice, she answered more sharply than normal.

"A few gravesites?" She frowned over her coffee. "You make it sound like a family plot we're digging into. To my knowledge, there are at least 150 archaeologically significant locations on this plateau alone, and those are just the ones we know of. Never mind the endangered wildlife here. This is all part of their heritage, so I can't blame them for being upset. No one understands the impact progress has on them."

Polzin was shaking his head, and he sighed with a half-smile, though his dark eyes held no trace of compassion.

"My dear Dr. Ramos, I brought you here because you have a scientific mind. Yet you speak like an impassioned member of Greenpeace. There are many graves here, but there are graves everywhere in this world. Some of them buried under cities. Can we save them all and save ourselves too? Of course not! This is more about superstitions. These people of the Altai, they worship mountains and streams, and cling to old ways out of ignorance and fear, and so they freeze and starve out here instead of accepting what the government wants to do to improve their lives. It is just so… how would you say it? So primitive, and uneducated. They refuse all outside help because they prefer to have discourse with spirits, trust visions, and fear evil eyes. We certainly wish to respect their beliefs, and we can do that best by recording for them what parts of their history we can find here before they are lost forever. But they just want the land left as is. You cannot expect that to happen in these modern times. Russia needs a stable economy to thrive as a country."

Marcela had already tuned him out. She did not share her current companion's disregard for the Altai people's unfortunate stubbornness. She would speak to the agitated natives and try to allay their fears. This was their land, so their concerns needed to be heard and addressed.

"Find me someone who speaks both English and their language, and I will talk to them tonight," she told Polzin, who simply shrugged.

"You will accomplish little. The government wants this project over soon, so that they can send surveyors and geologists in. They have been accommodating by bringing in an outside authority and shipping the finds to the United States, but that is as far as the funding will go."

She was about to interrupt but he raised a warning hand.

"There will be a gas pipeline through here whether these people want it or not," he added, and it was Marcela's turn to sigh. How many projects had she been called in on that were also time-sensitive because of conflicts between modern development and veneration of the area by locals?

"Why does it have to go through here specifically? Wasn't this declared a UNESCO World Heritage Site?"

Polzin rolled his eyes and rubbed the bristly beard on his chin. "That is a United Nations designation, but this is a matter of financial survival for our country. Natural gas is a very lucrative product, and we have a market eager for it. Many more people will have steady employment in a far more stable economy. Do not be so quick to judge us."

There was no sense in arguing with Polzin because he had made a few valid points, though she had begun to wonder what his stake in this enterprise was. Perhaps his government was actually paying him to expedite the removal of the mummy from the site, thinking it would make the protests go away. Marcela was determined to speak to the locals anyway, or she would leave on the next plane home.

"Call me when you have something set up. I'll be in my tent," she said, rising from the folding stool and stalking off.

Polzin watched her go with a frown.

~ ~ ~

It had not been a cordial meeting with the Altai people. There had been a litany of complaints and dire warnings, but Marcela had at least defused the situation.

In her tent that night, she crawled into her sleeping bag on the cot fully dressed, and tucked a wool blanket around her. She just could not shake the chill. Her mind was whirling with the events of the day, and then the tense meeting with the locals. She eventually fell into a troubled sleep.

~ ~ ~

The pain was excruciating. Her back was on fire. She could see nothing, because a great weight of icy darkness pressed down upon her. Her heart pounded wildly in her ears. She thrashed and tried to scream, but could neither move nor draw a breath. As the darkness pressed closer, she gasped desperately and frozen soil choked her—filling her mouth, nose, and eyes, pinning her arms and legs. The earth above lay heavily on her abdomen until she could no longer draw a breath...

Then it was cold, so cold. So dark and cold.

~ ~ ~

Marcela awoke with a shout, fighting to get free of her covers. She toppled onto the groundsheet of the tent, bruising her hip and left shoulder, gasping for air like someone who had been underwater too long.

Thankfully, it was only a dream. She extricated herself and pulling on her boots, got up to see if anyone had made coffee yet.

Later that morning she took a few of the Altai elders and a shaman to the site. She pointed out the amount of thawing that was going on.

"In time," she explained to them, "what is here will be lost to decay. If we remove what we find now, we can preserve and study it, and tell you what we know about your forebears. We can always return her to the earth when our work is done."

None of them liked the idea and the shaman was particularly unconvinced. "Never disturb the dead! If you move our ancestors," he warned her, "great evil will come forth. These people buried here were powerful ones in their time. Their spirits linger nearby, and they will fight back. Demons will spring from the darkness. It will be harmful for all of us—bad for your people and bad for mine. Already the spirits whisper their displeasure. Only I can hear them now, but soon all will know. Heed my warning while there is still time to undo the damage."

Marcela said some soothing words and ended the tour as soon as possible, but she was very troubled. She would not want her own ancestors exhumed and studied, so she understood the Altai people's anger and frustration. Still, her job was to serve the Russian government's needs, and they wanted her to get the mummy out of the country safely and soon. If she failed, some less skilled prehistorian would be brought in, and things would not be handled as well.

The necessary arrangements were made in an unprecedented accord between Russia and the U.S. America's involvement quashed the protests of the larger agencies. The equipment needed would be available. It was a once-in-a-lifetime opportunity for the Duwamish River Museum of Natural History, which was attached to Renton University's campus. It just had to get there intact.

~ ~ ~

For his part, Polzin was ecstatic. The Siberian mummy was heading to a U.S. museum to be analyzed and studied, and he was going with it.

~ ~ ~

It had been a hectic couple of days and yet they had accomplished much. After the site was sketched and everything cataloged and removed, they had been able to loosen the ice block almost intact and it was wrapped and crated. A crane to remove it had not been available but someone had brought in MI-26 transport helicopter. The scaffolding and cover was removed, and straps were attached to the well-wrapped ice block so it could be lifted free from its cold gravesite.

Suddenly the ground began to shake again. Dirt and rocks slumped back into the pit. Unbalanced people fell in with it while others scrambled to safety. Some ran around securing camp materials and extinguishing lanterns and propane stoves. Tents went down as a blast of icy wind shook the copter.

"We warned you!" one of the local shamans called from behind the security perimeter. "The spirits are angry!"

The tremor ended, and the helicopter moved in again. The crated remains were lifted and traveled many miles to a highway where the refrigerated truck awaited. Marcela and Polzin followed it to oversee the crate's storage on the truck. They talked low and quietly, both of them a bit shaken by the sudden tremor.

"There have been earthquakes here before," he reassured her. "We know of a major fault area. This was just a tremor—nothing more."

"It was well-timed," Marcela commented.

"A coincidence of natural means," he insisted. "No spirits control that." She wondered if he said that to convince her or himself.

While loading the truck, there was another mishap. As they were lowering the frozen block down to the ramp, one of the straps from the copter suddenly parted. The wrapped block of ice tilted drunkenly and began to slide free, smashing into a man who attempted to steady it as the heavy object came down. He howled in pain, suffering a compound fracture of the left arm with bruised or cracked ribs. Another man was whipped in the face by the free end of the severed strap, and it was feared that he might lose an eye. They had to wait on site for a medic to treat them, before it was decided that they'd both be driven by one of the government ministers to the nearest hospital.

Once the ice block with the mummy was loaded and the truck was ready to go, the rest of them piled into a military motorcade which drove slowly back to Barnaul airport, where a chartered U.S. flight to Seattle would be waiting. They had been assured that the baggage area temperature would not thaw the remains, and that it would be loaded and unloaded as priority, and quickly put into refrigeration upon arrival.

Even the long ride to the airport had its mishaps. A few miles down the highway there was a detour due to an accident ahead. A crevasse had opened and a couple of vehicles had become trapped. While negotiating the detour, the motorcade got separated from the truck bearing the mummy, which took a wrong turn. They had to wait for it to catch up. Later on, there was an accident within the motorcade itself, where brakes failed and several vehicles rear-ended each other right before an exit. Injuries were minor, but that slowed progress considerably while things were sorted out.

Marcela was grateful she had insisted on the refrigerated vehicle, and that the plane would not leave without them.

"This is turning out to be a very costly venture," Polzin complained.

"In many ways, yes," Marcela agreed. He was likely thinking of monetary expenditures, but Marcela Ramos was concerned about people who had been injured. She had been on dig sites before where there were injuries and mechanical failures, but most of them were due to human error. This was just bizarre.

The rest of the trip was uneventful except for a few stops to let wildlife cross the highway.

"You see?" Polzin said as they waited to board, watching the well-wrapped artifact going into the jet's hold. "She will be given

VIP treatment. Our Siberian passenger will be off the plane long before we disembark."

"Let's hope so," Marcela commented wearily. It would be a long flight and she was eager to get home. She was still dealing with disturbing dreams that woke her from restless sleep once or twice each night, and even in the daytime she had the prickling feeling of being watched or followed. At times she swore someone or something was stalking her. Polzin seemed somewhat antsy too, though he said nothing much about it. She hoped to be able to grab some shut-eye on the plane because she was dragging.

In between mishaps she had gone over her notes, thinking about the presentations she had given. The UNESCO people and the international wildlife preservation groups had not been too hard to deal with, because they understood that the archaeologists were not their enemies—the placement of the pipeline was.

Meeting one last time with the area elders, though, had been strained at best. The same people told her bitterly that she was damning them and herself by being involved.

"Altai is alive, and we who live here are part of it," the Shaman with them insisted. "This land will fight for what you are raping from the soil. Our ancestral dead are the guardians of the gates to the underworld. You will live to regret this decision, Dr. Ramos."

In some ways, she already did.

~ ~ ~

The dreams became even more disturbing on the long flight. Marcela was bone tired, so she tried to doze off, but discordant images of warfare wakened her. And then there was the voice...

She could not understand it, but it was female, angry, and insistent. The words were reminiscent of a Turkic language. The meaning was clear enough. "Take me home!"

I'm going out of my mind!

There were two stop-overs—a brief one in Moscow and a longer one at JFK, where they were delayed due to rainy weather and some paperwork issues over the nature of the cargo and Polzin's traveler's visa. They wound up booking the mummy on another cargo flight, and catching a later plane for themselves. They had time to leave the airport by cab and eat at a deli that Marcela favored.

"You look very tired," Polzin told her over a late breakfast of bagels and bialys with good strong coffee. Marcela nodded around a bite covered with lox and cream cheese and swallowed with a sip of coffee.

"I haven't been sleeping well," she admitted. "I've had too many strange dreams lately."

"As have I. The excitement of this find is overwhelming, and the mind plays tricks." He sounded evasive. She looked up at him quizzically.

"Are you sure that's all this is?" she asked in a low voice. "These dreams are… frightening."

Polzin turned a little pale as he sipped his own coffee—black with three spoons of sugar—but his voice remained level. "I am a scientist, as are you, Marcela. My training says ancient curses and demons from the underworld are the stuff of fiction and B movies. A mummy is simply a dead body that has been preserved to the specifications of some culture's spiritual beliefs. They control nothing."

Marcela thought back to her Catholic upbringing, and the veneration of saints through their relics. It had all seemed very real when she was a girl, and it was hard to put that feeling aside even as an adult who had spent many years evaluating the world around her by the scientific method. She touched the chain around her neck and drew up the cross, which gave her a small sense of comfort.

"Have you no spiritual beliefs of your own then?" she asked Lyov.

"Should I?" he answered all too quickly. "Oh, I was raised in the tradition of the Moscow Patriarchate—what you would call Russian Orthodox. My grandparents were Estonian and they were sent to the labor camps for their stubborn beliefs. My parents saw their church destroyed and their priest imprisoned, yet they still believed. As for me, I wanted an education, and had to sacrifice any public worship so that I could go to school and become a scientist who rediscovers our roots. In university I learned the truth—that governments control all faith. I have not bothered with it since."

"How sad," she said, thinking of the peacefulness of attending mass with her family around her. Polzin was about to retort when Marcela's cell phone went off, and she held up a hand. She had a hurried conversation with someone on the other end, and then got to her feet.

"We need to find a cab and get back to the airport immediately. There's been an accident loading the mummy crate, and someone was killed."

She threw down some cash on the table and they both hurried out to the street.

~ ~ ~

The story was puzzling. The handlers who were overseeing the mummy crate's transfer into the belly of the cargo jet were moving it up the conveyor ramp when a horde of some small rodents issued from within and began swarming all over the men, squealing and biting. The witnesses were all in agreement, there were hundreds of the creatures. Someone panicked and tried to stop the conveyor but he must have hit the wrong lever, and it backed up rapidly, pinning a man at the end and crushing his skull.

Marcela and Polzin were questioned separately for the better part of an hour. They had to give statements to both police and FAA inspectors before the authorities would allow the crate onto the plane. They came close to missing their own flight because of it. They were not allowed in to inspect their cargo until after the accident scene was cleaned up and the body removed.

Polzin was livid.

"This is an outrage! There were no vermin in the frozen hole we took this from, nor was there any on the plane. I checked everything myself! You must have an infestation here. I want to see the airport commissioner right now!"

He stomped off with a guard, so it was Marcela who checked things over. The crate around the well-wrapped ice block was damaged and there were still traces of blood on it, but the contents were intact and frozen. She made sure the wrappings inside were in good shape. There was absolutely no sign of any creature within, nothing on the conveyor or in the truck it had been unloaded from, and none from the belly of the plane it was going into. Yet several witnesses on the scene described them vividly as small, jumping mice.

Perhaps they were drawn by the smell? She had no other theory. The whispering in her head grew stronger the longer she remained near it, and was accompanied by the harsh laugh of a female voice.

Laughing at me I suppose, she thought with a shudder.

Marcela was exhausted by the time they made it back to their own terminal and were hustled off to be boarded. She had a sick feeling at the pit of her stomach that this would not be the last unfortunate incident that ended in a death.

The passenger flight was fairly smooth and routine. But the cargo plane reported several episodes of severe turbulence and engine trouble toward the end of the flight. There were wails, shrieks and groans from the cargo area, and the cabin lights had flickered several times. Never was it so good to have a routine delivery over, but when Sea-Tac came in sight and the crew began their approach, the landing gear had stuck, and they had to circle so that the ground crews had time to clear the runway area. The cargo jet eventually came down safely, but some stormy weather was kicking up so it was a fight to keep the craft level with the resulting wind shear. The cargo pilot was well seasoned, but even he was rattled by the time they taxied up to their assigned bay.

"Get that thing off my plane," he demanded as he disembarked, the rest of the crew having already left. "And check this baby over carefully. I've never had so much trouble in one flight."

"Where are you off to?" one of the mechanics asked.

He walked away rapidly without looking back. "I'm either tendering my resignation and then getting drunk," he said, "or I'm going to find a priest and have him bless the gremlins out of that bird!"

~ ~ ~

Marcela read the reports for the third time, shaking her head.

Not only had the crew who flown the mummy from JFK to Sea-Tac reported strange noises and mysterious mechanical issues, but so had the trucking company that picked it up. In fact, they'd had to send a second truck when the first one had an engine fire. And now that they had the mummy in the basement of the museum, where a climate controlled study room had been created, the perplexing occurrences had escalated.

Within hours of bringing it in for the slow thaw, strange noises were coming from the basement. The technicians overseeing the thawing process had to be rotated out every couple hours because of physical complaints of persistent fevers and chills that caused hallucinations. One woman was rushed to the hospital with chest pains after she claimed to have been stalked by a large cat of some kind. She abruptly quit the following day.

A curator and exhibit designer with her staff were working on the first floor late into the evening before a gallery show opened. The five of them heard rhythmic sounds like singing coming from the service elevator. When they called security to check it, the elevator was in the basement and refused to come up. The noise was shrugged off as something that had gone haywire with the mechanism. A repair crew called in the morning found nothing wrong with it, but it continued to periodically malfunction.

One of the interns had some kind of meltdown. "She speaks to me," he said tearfully as security guards pried a tissue sampling implement from his hands and led him away. He'd threatened to stab anyone who touched the desiccated body. "I can't understand what she's saying, but she wants me to take her somewhere on horseback. I don't even know how to ride!" He sobbed and thrashed in their grip as they hauled him away before he hurt himself. Someone was already on the phone with the local hospital, and a siren was soon heard wailing outside.

The disturbances continued. Long-stored items suddenly turned up in odd places. The sounds of armed conflict replete with galloping horses, the clash of arms, and screams of the dying were randomly broadcast through listening stations at various exhibits and over the public address system. Very rapid blasts of arctic wind swept through galleries crowded with onlookers. The museum had to cancel most of the evening workshops and flashlight tours because the lights would not stay on reliably.

None of these things had happened before they brought the mummy in. It was also notable that people who came in regular contact with the remains tended to become very ill, or paranoid that they were being watched by something. All of it taken together was just too much coincidence for even the most skeptical amongst them, and whispers of a "curse" started making their way through the ranks of the under-staff. It became impossible to keep anyone on the project.

It was beyond bizarre. So were the ongoing dreams, which now affected Marcela during the day. Anytime she took a breather to clear her head, the images flashed around her. In fact, they were more than just random scenes, but actual sensory details of some other life. They were so vivid, so exhilarating and yet frightening, she sometimes had trouble dragging her mind back to the present world. Whenever she closed her eyes, she was back there again.

~ ~ ~

Galloping hard across the open steppe with the rush of the wind in her face, she sensed the lathered hide of the horse sliding over muscles that bunched and stretched beneath her. Her heart pounded wildly as the war cries went up, lungs burning as she gasped frigid air, determined to take the lead as they plunged down slope. Snarling in defiance, she raised a spear and smashed into the front line of those who rode just as hard to meet them. The chaos of battle erupted on all sides. Surrounded by shouting, grunting warriors, she focused on who among them were friends and who were foes.

The sudden lunge of an enemy too near almost threw her from her mount! An overtaxed mind registered the threat nearly too late, but battle nerves and well-honed skill lifted the small shield automatically to block the blow. Digging heels into the horse's flank, she drove the enemy warrior backward. A thrust and sideways rip, and he went down off his mount. *Unfortunately the spear went with him. She pulled her spare, sighted another target, and rode him down.*

Her horse was kicked by another and then injured by a quick spear thrust to the flank, but the gelding was game and staggered onward, dodging the writhing bodies below. She had to get free of the throng to use the bow. All around her came the screams of wounded equines and the agonized cries of injured men. The iron smell of blood and the stench of death filled her nostrils, with the whirling dark wings of the carrion birds overhead as she urged her mount through the press.

The spear that took her off her mount went deep into the horse's gullet. With a screech, the animal staggered and fell while she threw herself free in order not to be pinned beneath it. She was able to get a couple arrows into her would-be captors before someone knocked her senseless. She knew no more until she was brought before their chieftain.

~ ~ ~

Another scene of the past had somehow threaded its way into her consciousness before Marcela shook it off. She was sleeping in snatches, because the nightmares would wake her up multiple times.

Polzin also appeared frazzled, his eyes feverishly bright in dark-circled sockets. He had become alternately morose and bombastic, one moment berating the team for their slowness in thawing the body, next begging them to be careful.

"We must learn all we can from her," he insisted, his knuckles white as he grasped a tablet one-handed and paged through notes. The two of them were walking wrecks. The long, tedious hours were getting to them.

Eventually the surface ice was gone, and while the mummy was being kept in a super-cooled chamber, they could examine her at length. Most of her skin had been preserved, though whatever had been left of her clothing had moldered and decomposed. There were scars on her back and buttocks and her eyes, nostrils, and mouth were filled with soil. Other than that, she bore no serious wounds—certainly nothing that should have ended her life. Something about that didn't seem right, but Marcela couldn't put her finger on it.

They might have to bring in a forensic anthropologist to determine what exactly had killed the mummified woman.

Tattoos on her arms held everyone in awe, for they were amazingly detailed. Unlike the famous 1993 find, these markings were more akin to what male warriors decorated themselves with. Battle scenes on horseback and predators taking prey along with healed wounds told Marcela that this was a woman who fought beside men as an equal.

"I'd like to get her scanned," she told Polzin one day during a break where they were comparing notes. "I have a hunch this was no ordinary woman of the era."

"Really?" he said with candor. "What makes you say so?"

She turned on him almost defensively, and replied in a clipped tone, "Her interment was hasty and unremarkable, and while her body shows old scars of battle, she was in good health at the time of her death. I want to know what killed her and why she died dishonored."

"You Americans have all the money," he scoffed with a laugh. "Scan her for whatever you like."

~ ~ ~

While they were waiting for the results of the CT scan, Marcela asked the university for a sabbatical so she could spend more time at the museum. She and Polzin began to work together in the basement most days, feverishly trying to uncover the secrets of the Altai mummy. They went over the team's notes and then weighed, measured, and recorded the desiccated body's general condition before getting more deeply into the examination.

"She's remarkably preserved," Marcela said through her mask as she gently turned the frigid husk of the woman this way and that, looking over the tattoos and other ritual markings. "I'd say her body froze before it could begin to decompose."

"Yes, the lower average temperature at the time kept the permafrost deep," Polzin said, his voice rather muffled by his own mask. "I see those scars you mentioned." He pointed to them.

"Yet it doesn't appear that she died in battle," Marcela countered.

"What makes you say that?" he queried.

"No mortal wound." She turned the body over carefully, and then stopped and examined her back.

"What is it?" Polzin asked.

"This," she said. Marcela traced some scored lines on the leathery skin on the mummy's back with a gloved forefinger. Her forehead below the cold suit's protective hood was lined in concentration. "Why was this not mentioned in your notes?"

"I assumed they were postmortem cracking of the skin from the freezing temperatures," Polzin asked as he pointed down at a network of skin fissures. "Her back was on the ice, after all.

She shook her head. "I don't believe so, though it's hard to tell because of the shrinkage. Yet they're ridged and appear almost in an X-shaped pattern, and there's grit imbedded in them." She ran a finger very gently into one of the more open sections. "I'd hazard a guess they were open cuts at the time she was interred."

"What would make such a pattern of wounds?" he said quizzically.

Marcela recalled the jumbled images from the recurring dreams, and a shudder ran through her. That part always began with her back feeling like it was on fire.

"A flogging is what I would suspect," she said quietly. "It was not healed when she died, if this grit tests of subsoil particles from the grave area as I suspect. I'll have samples taken of it to be matched with the pit soil. There's plenty in her mouth and nostrils too."

"What is your hypothesis of her death then?" Polzin asked her rather crossly. His impatience suggested to Marcela that he was growing jealous of her knowledge and ability to unravel the mystery of the ice maiden.

"I'll wait for the CT scan results before I bias your opinion." Marcela once again had that prickling feeling someone or something was watching and judging her. The room was refrigerator cold, and their workspace was zero degrees Fahrenheit, but she shivered in her protective suit at the thought of what this woman went through in her short but eventful life.

I have to get this right.

~ ~ ~

The night security guard had his feet up and was idly watching the building's floor monitors while enjoying his snack when he thought he saw something moving around in the basement. He sat up straight and brought the basement camera into sharper focus. It might have just been a glitch because there shouldn't have been anyone down there this evening. The team working on the new mummy had all left earlier.

Checking the recorded footage showed him little. While the camera panned the stairs, a nearby service elevator and the fire exit, there were too many things in the way to do a reliable scan of the entire area. He squinted at the basement monitor, trying to make out something fleeting that rippled the shadows on the recording. He was shaking his head when it happened again.

These were strange, fluid motions of a darker shade that appeared solid in the gloom, so they weren't camera "ghosts." Whatever it was didn't trip the motion sensors on the security lights, but it had to be an intruder. The fire door alarm never went off, so somebody must have hidden in one of the upstairs rooms till after closing time and then slipped past while he was on one of his rounds. Could be just a couple of teenagers looking for a creepy place to go necking, or a homeless person seeking a cool spot to sleep at the end of a hot day. His snack set aside, he stood up and made sure he had his flashlight, baton, and cell phone, and sighed unhappily. It would be best go check it out, because if anything got stolen or damaged, he'd get sacked.

The service elevator was not working again, so he took the stairs. The farther he descended, the more the hair on the back of his neck stood on end. He had an eerie feeling he was being watched, and it didn't help that it was so blasted cold down there he shivered in his short-sleeved uniform shirt. He knew the basement was kept cool and dry because it helped preserve specimens and artifacts, but this was biting cold—like a winter day up in the mountains. He began to shiver, which turned the nervous sweat on his body into icy rivulets trickling down beneath his clothing.

He had to wind his way into shadowy pockets between racks and shelves, piles of boxes, worktables, and support columns. He could hear something padding around in the far left hand corner of the workspace, which was where the mummy room was. Stories whispered by nervous staff over breakroom coffee came back to mind, but he fought off the nibbling fears. It was all nonsense.

Then the chanting started. It was a low-toned woman's voice, full of longing, anger, and contempt. It seemed to come from everywhere and nowhere, and it was soft in volume, though the sounds were harsh and guttural, some almost like a growl, others like the sighing of the wind or the far off scream of birds of prey high in the air. It was like nothing he'd ever heard before, and his blood ran cold.

He shone the flashlight around, and called out in a gruff but shaking voice, "Who's down here? Show yourself or I'm calling the police!" The voice always seemed to be where the beam of light wasn't. Something stalked around behind him and there was a snarl, but when he whirled, nothing was there. Feverishly, he pulled his baton and backed toward the stairs, but his feet entangled in one of the racks and he fell, dropping the flashlight and his only weapon. The flashlight went out, and the room became pitch black.

Something *was* down there—something that did not belong, something not of this world. He was sure of it. The chanting grew louder, and added to it were the sounds of dancing feet in some sort of stomping rhythm. A long-bodied, sinuous creature circled around him. He could hear it padding on the concrete floor, smell its fetid animal stench, see its glowing eyes watching him in the darkness. The droning vocalizations went on, with added yips and answering growls. The creature came ever closer. He could feel the hot breath on the side of his face as it snapped at him and hissed.

Back against a wall, he dug out his cell phone with shaking hands, but the battery was dead and it would not even light up. He was so cold and stiff, he wanted to just lie down and rest, but he feared the wild animal would attack him if he did. Shakily, he regained his feet and with chattering teeth, lurched around wildly in the darkness, trying to find the stairs. He wandered through the basement for more than an hour, hounded by the chanting and the restless movements of the creature pacing him. He never found the stairwell, and eventually collapsed in despair, almost in tears.

There was the sound of a bow being drawn, the slight twanging noise of an arrow, and something went deep into his chest wall. He gasped for breath, clutching what felt like a feathered shaft protruding from his ribcage. The pain was overwhelming. The last lamenting sounds of the chant faded away as he gave a few labored breaths before he lay still and rigid, cold with death.

They found him in the morning not far from the stairs, his face contorted with horror, his eyes wide open, hands clutching at his chest. Not a wound on him, and the medical examiner said it was likely a heart attack. They'd know more after an autopsy.

And they found the mummy in the super-cooled chamber. It had somehow turned itself over to face the door of its enclosure, and its lips had curled into a grim smile.

~ ~ ~

"A terrible medical tragedy for this man and his family, but nothing more," was Polzin's answer to the small group of employees who buttonholed him, demanding answers. "Dr. Ramos is in a better position to answer your questions than I am." He pushed past them on his way into the inner office, and shut the door. Marcela had to deal with them when she came in, calming the fears and answering their questions as honestly as she could. She was furious with her colleague for not standing by her.

The museum's board of directors was also looking for answers, because the bad press could prompt a few donors to pull back their contributions. Polzin met with them privately while Marcela was dealing with the edgy staff. When questioned about the Altai mummy project's reputation for accidents and mishaps, he shrugged it off.

"I do not see a firm connection, other than in the minds of the credulous. The unfortunate man who died down there last night was very much out of shape and well into his sixties. With the service elevator out, he had to take the stairs. The company who hired him should be answering these questions, not me."

"Many employees and interns have reported odd phenomena since the mummy was brought in. What do you make of that?" asked a women who had been reading complaint transcripts. She glanced up over her reading glasses at him, frowning. "I warn you, we will be looking into this."

"As you should! People who work in research capacities cannot afford to be so impressionable. I suggest you screen your people more thoroughly so that such sensational rumors do not become the basis of mass hysteria. Now please, Dr. Ramos and I have important work to do..." Polzin politely but firmly took his leave.

He might have been able to shrug off the current death in a string of clandestine calamities, but Marcela Ramos was extremely troubled. There had been no dreams the night before, and she had felt relieved when her alarm went off that she'd finally slept soundly. Then the call came while she was on her way to work. Now this informal inquest...

"We need to wrap this up and return the remains to the Altai," she insisted later, when they were alone, but Polzin would not hear of it.

"After all the trouble we went through to get it here!" he snapped in exasperation. "Do you have any idea how rare it is for there to be such cooperation between your country and mine? I would be the laughingstock of my colleagues if I gave up so easily and returned to Russia over some foolish superstition. No, Marcela, I insist that it remains here. And if you don't wish to be involved, I will find another partner."

She shook her head in wonder. He was so driven. "Lyov... several people have been injured, and two have died."

"And how is this the fault of a seventh-century woman's mummified body?" he countered scornfully.

"You have to trust me on this," she said as she suited up to head into what the museum staff referred to as the "meat locker." "Whatever you choose to believe, this mummy belongs back where it came from."

She took two steps into the room and stopped suddenly. "Oh God..." she said when she saw the position the mummy was in, and crossed herself. "Lyov, her eyes are open and she's... she's grinning!"

"Someone must have tampered with the display," he insisted, but he was terribly pale as he came over to her angle to view the desiccated corpse. "This is an outrage! I will have their jobs, heads will roll—"

He never finished what he was saying.

~ ~ ~

Polzin took one look at the mummy's face, and he understood what his own dreams meant. At that moment, he knew what had to be done.

He had not dreamed about the warrior woman who was trapped in the icy grave. He had dreamed of how she got there—by whom, and why. So while he worked with Marcela that day, trying to unravel the mummy's secrets, his mind was racing with the possibilities that entailed.

He had no true contacts here in America, but someone amongst the Russian expatriates would know where he could get what he needed to set things right.

~ ~ ~

That evening, after everyone had gone home, Marcela set her glasses down, sat back in her chair, and raised her arms over her head. She closed her eyes and arched her back, stretching tired muscles cramped from spending half the day crouched over the mummy case, and the other half hunched over her keyboard, noting her findings.

There weren't many revelations. The results of the CT scan and DNA tests were in, and they more or less rubber-stamped what she already suspected. The mummified woman was of mixed European and Asian heritage and once cross-checked, her genetic code resembled that of samples taken from late Iron Age Scythian graves in the Altai of Mongolia. What little could be told of her cause of death verified what Marcela had already suspected.

She had been buried alive. Very much alive, in an unmarked grave. That spoke of great hostility by her aggressors. She'd been beaten first, and was practically naked at the time, hence the lack of fiber material. Still, she fought to free herself, for there was dirt under her ragged nails. The CT scan showed some of the older wounds on her body that had healed—the indication of other battles fought in earlier times. She was somewhere between twenty-five and twenty-eight, and had never given birth. Her skeleton and what they could see of her muscles showed that she had trained hard from an early age. Perhaps this woman was one of Herodotus' fabled Amazons, the warrior women who allegedly fought battles and scorned men.

Marcela felt sort of a kinship with the Altai mummy, for while the professor was far from a warrior herself, she had learned to fight for her right to be acknowledged in a field often dominated by men. Even with more than a decade of field experience, three successful books, numerous conference and lecture engagements, she still struggled for acceptance and respect from her male peers. Polzin was just the latest in a long line of condescending colleagues. Oh, they were polite enough and often willing to let her do the lion's share of the work, but at the very least they insisted upon equal credit for her painstaking research. Most of them wanted to be the one who presented the findings. In fact, several had gone to the press before the official release with a tidbit soundbite that usurped her later announcement.

She had been furious each time it happened, but initially shrugged it off as the price you paid to climb the ladder toward success. In these latter years, she was not so accommodating. So that was why, when Polzin had begun to insert himself between her and her fellowship at the museum, she became increasingly wary of him.

I should have been the one meeting with the board, not Lyov. He's an *outsider. What is he up to?*

She would soon find out.

~ ~ ~

Marcela could not put a finger on what exactly drew her back down to the basement room at the end of that day. She felt compelled to have one more look at the woman who had died over 2600 years ago. Perhaps it was her strong Catholic upbringing, but she couldn't help thinking that the mummy had been found for some purpose that perhaps only God understood—even if this woman's people didn't share the same concept of deity.

She punched in the code and unlocked the door, verifying that the interior key card was still on the lanyard around her neck before entering—it wouldn't be good to get locked in without protective gear. She slipped inside and stood in her lab coat, hugging her shoulders and stamping her feet against the cold, wondering what other secretsthe long-dead body held. What had this young woman's short life been like, other than the endless training and fighting? Did she have friends? Lovers? Wear on her femur and pelvis showed that from an early age she had often been on horseback. That agreed with the dreams Marcela had of plains riding battles. She had to step outside her scientific training to wrap her brain around the totality of the message the desiccated body held.

They were actually somewhat alike—both so dedicated to what they believed in and determined to succeed that they remained unpartnered with no children at an age when most women of their respective eras would be raising families. Marcela understood on a deep level what drove this woman to devote her life to perfecting her talents. She went back over the dream images, trying to make sense of them.

"What have you been trying to tell me?" Marcela whispered through chattering teeth.

There was no answer. No flickering lights, strange noises, or furtive shadow movement. Just the persistent cold rumbling of the refrigeration unit and that feeling of being watched and evaluated. She shook her head, turned and scanned her card, and left the mummy room. Locking the outer door again, she headed for the stairs.

~ ~ ~

Polzin met her on her way up. "I tried your cellphone, but it went directly to voicemail," he said in way of greeting.

"I was down in back, and the reception isn't great there. I'm surprised to see you here tonight," she added cautiously. What was he doing in the museum this late? He had complained of a headache and left early.

"I have some things I want to go over with you," he answered quietly, but with a bit of an edge to his voice. He was blocking the stairs, and she wanted to go back up.

"Let's talk in my office," she suggested, and he shook his head and started coming down the stairwell toward her.

"I would prefer we remain down here where we can examine our Altai warrior woman. If my theory proves correct, we may have a breakthrough. I have to demonstrate what I am thinking, but I forgot my keycard at the hotel. Do you have yours?"

"Right here," she pointed to the lanyard on her neck, and he nodded with a slight smile. She noticed that he already had lab gloves on. Was that odd?

"Very good, then. Shall we go have another look?" His voice trailed off as she sighed in resignation and turned to head back down the stairs. Polzin was fumbling with something in his pocket and his breath came fast. When they got to the bottom of the staircase he put his hand on her arm and gently but firmly steered her back toward the mummy room, out of sight of the security camera, in case it reactivated.

"And your theory is?" she said rather wearily, with a touch of irritation in her voice. He was being so dramatic.

"Only that women should know their place in a man's world," Polzin said as he jabbed the first injection into Marcela's thigh. When she whirled on him, he twisted her arm back behind her painfully. She squirmed and the second injection plunged into an ample hip.

"What have you done?" she gasped as a wave of nausea hit her. Her heart began to race and she was sweating profusely. "What was that? Drugs?"

Polzin laughed. "I am no fool. That would be too obvious," he said with a mirthless laugh. "This is simply an epinephrine injector used for allergic reactions." He held out a third one, which she tried to bat at, before he jabbed it into her other thigh and she groaned and nearly collapsed. "Even if they notice the marks, they will think you overdosed yourself. Which is why when they find your body down here, they will believe you had some sort of frightening hallucination due to your physical state."

Polzin shoved her along before him. Marcela reeled drunkenly and gasped for breath, her head swimming and her chest cramping from the excess adrenaline that was making her heart pound like war drums. While Polzin punched in the code that unlocked the cold room door from the outside, she just couldn't orient herself enough to fight back. Then she had a nose bleed.

Please, not a cerebral hemorrhage!

"Goodbye, Dr. Ramos. I will be sure to express my shock and grief appropriately when they tell me of your untimely death. Perhaps they will even let me read your eulogy. Certainly the university will be grateful if I volunteer to continue your work here. Perhaps in time I will obtain a fellowship."

"Lyov—don't do this!" she gasped out as he ripped away the lanyard with the keycard that would release the door from the inside before he flung her into the refrigerated room.

"Sorry, but I do not need you anymore," he answered in an indifferent tone. He let the door slam shut behind her, punched in the locking code, and walked away, leaving a gasping and freezing Marcela alone in the darkness with the mummy.

She collapsed on the cold floor, shivering and miserable. Her heart pounded furiously, her breath came in frosty gulps of supercooled air that burned her lungs, and her head pounded so fiercely it felt like her brain would explode through her skull. The adrenaline would not last long but it would tire her out, and if she didn't have a heart attack or a stroke, when it wore off, hypothermia would make her catatonic. She cursed herself for insisting that they remove the intercom system from the room to stop the strange noises from reaching the museum floor.

Marcela tried to rise but her quivering limbs refused to hold her, and she scrabbled around helplessly. She couldn't even get her voice above a whisper, she was so short of breath.

"I don't want to die here!" she lamented feebly.

Then do not give in to weakness—fight to live! something shouted in her mind. It was not in any language she had ever heard, but somehow it became understandable. Chaotic images flashed of warfare and the camaraderie of other women dressed for battle and splashed with blood; visions of riding hard across frozen plains and through snow; of bows twanging, spears being launched, and bodies falling. *You fight in this world, or you die and the enemy wins.*

"H-help…m-me…" Marcela begged through chattering teeth, as she made it to her knees but could not rise.

Find strength within your anger, sister, was all the help she got.

"Get me out of this mess, and I'll see that you are returned to your home," Marcela pleaded.

~ ~ ~

Lyov Polzin was a man who did not leave much to chance, and so he had planned well. He had parked his rental vehicle in the crowded student commons lot and skulked over through the landscaping behind the buildings. The employee keycard lifted from the desk of the museum librarian earlier that day got him into the side delivery door of the cafeteria area without alerting anyone. The guard station was right down the hall. Deactivating the security camera was fairly simple. He waited until the new night guard was out on her rounds, and simply set the system up to replay the loop from the day before. That and the woman's unfamiliarity with the museum layout bought him enough time to make it down to the basement.

The gloves would leave no fingerprints. He could get rid of the epipens somewhere later. All he had to do now was drop Dr. Ramos' keycard somewhere obvious and remove himself from the premises via the back hallways where he would not be seen. The librarian's keycard would get him out the door again.

The delivery door refused to open. The librarian's keycard had somehow become damaged in his pocket, and it didn't release the lock. He had already dropped Marcela's card down the basement stairs and there was no way he'd dare go back after it with the guard making her rounds. Desperately, he headed to a service door on the opposite side of the building, but that also refused to open. He was tempted to jiggle it, but it might set off an alarm.

There were footsteps coming! Polzin ducked and hurried down the next hallway, keeping his head low, hoping the security camera in the area was panning the other way. The footsteps were getting louder. It had to be the guard—damn her! He dodged through the North American Mammal displays, and into the room with the Ice Age Megafauna, trying to remain unseen between the great creatures without knocking something over in the dark. The footsteps kept coming.

He was about to head into the Native American Encampment room, when something off to the right growled from the shadows. He backed up and then the footsteps stopped, and instead there was a padding of big paws on the tile floor. Something else was stalking him…

He turned to run, and fell face down after two steps when the weight of a large body knocked him flat. There were snarls, and a few rumbling growls. He twisted onto his back, and fought with fists and feet, trying to get upright, but the big creature would not let him.

"No, no, no! Nothing is alive in here!" he yelled as the fetid smell of a carnivore's reeking breath swept over him and he felt the jaws clamp down on his exposed throat. His scream of terror and agony turned to a bubbling whine as fangs ripped through his jugular and carotid, and hot arterial blood sprayed everywhere.

And then there was nothing… no pain, no feeling at all, no sound except for the crunching of flesh and bone, and the mocking voice of a woman.

You go to the underworld to join the man who took my life.

~ ~ ~

It was the furtive sound of someone slipping through the hallways before her that led the new security guard to the basement entrance. She found a staff keycard pass where it had somehow gotten caught on the basement railing. A noise in the far corner made her draw her weapon and advance slowly. There she found a disheveled and freezing Marcela Ramos banging on the door to the mummy room with a wooden stool.

"Give me the code and I'll let you out," the guard shouted, holstering her gun.

After a series of shouts back and forth, the door opened and a very cold and grateful Marcela Ramos collapsed in the other woman's arms. An ambulance was called and she went off to the hospital to be treated for mild hypothermia.

Unfortunately the door didn't close properly, and in the ensuing excitement no one noticed. The police had been called in because Marcela insisted her Russian colleague had assaulted her and trapped her in the refrigerated room. They spread out through the museum and the grounds outside, hunting him.

They found Lyov Polzin dead of an apparent accident. Somehow he had knocked down a smilodon model and the long curved teeth of the saber-toothed cat lacerated his throat when he tried to move out from under it. He bled out in minutes, but the look of horror frozen on his face said he'd panicked.

Marcela's story checked out, because Polzin still had the lab gloves on and the used epipens in his pocket. His body was turned over to the Russian embassy, with a stern but diplomatic warning that in the future, any foreign nationals sent to work on scientific research in the U.S. would have to pass both a drug screening and a mental health test. The people from the local consulate denied any knowledge of his actions and expressed shocked disbelief that the archeologist would have attacked his American colleague.

Fortunately, other than some minor frostbite and extreme exhaustion, Marcela was found to be in good health. She was able to go back to work the next day, with the idea of finishing her notes on the Altai mummy. Unfortunately, the refrigeration unit for the mummy room had overheated because of the door being ajar, and it malfunctioned. The Siberian warrior woman's body decomposed to the point where further study became impossible.

There were no more dreams now, no strange noises or feelings of being watched and evaluated. No contact whatsoever with the spirit of the mummified woman. Whatever her reasons had been for troubling those around her, it was over. She had moved beyond. Marcela Ramos was certain of that.

The museum, at Marcela's request, repacked the remains and she accompanied them home to the windswept steppe a week later.

A solemn group of elders from the Altai village along with someone from the Russian government escorted the body back to the Ukok Plateau. No one asked Marcela why she insisted on coming along, nor was she bothered about the possibility of a pipeline or global warming ruining the area for further exploration. She could not speak of the things that had transpired, for both the museum's board of directors and someone from the government had debriefed her before she left. The less said about the matter, the better.

"We knew," said the shaman she had spoken to when she had last been there, "that Polzin was a government operative sent here. He tried to force us to give up the Altai, and deny the souls of our ancestors and take our spiritual foundation away. Money talks to those who have black hearts, but they pay for it in the end."

Marcela nodded as she watched the small casket of native larch holding the remains lowered into the reopened grave. She now understood her purpose in the adventure that had almost cost her own life.

She needed me to prevent the desecration of her homeland. I hope she rests easy now.

Marcela Ramos' life would never be the same.

OUR ARCHAEOLOGY STAFF

Bruening, John C.

John C. Bruening, a thirty-year veteran of journalism, editing, publishing and marketing, is a co-founder and an editor at Flinch Books. His 2016 debut novel, *The Midnight Guardian: Hour of Darkness*, has been described as "a Republic serial set to prose" (Ron Fortier, Pulp Fiction Reviews) and "the creative construct of a first-rate storyteller" (William Patrick Maynard, Black Gate). The jury's still out on "The Warrior and the Stone," his contribution to *Restless*, but he prefers to think of it as something akin to an Indiana Jones tale written by Robert E. Howard. By the time these words are printed, John will be working on various upcoming Flinch projects, including the second adventure in the Midnight Guardian saga, which is scheduled for release in the latter part of 2018. He lives in a suburb of Cleveland, Ohio, with his wife, his two teenage children, a good-natured collie and a temperamental cat.

Gafford, Sam

Sam Gafford has been published in a variety of anthologies and publications. His fiction has appeared in such collections as *Black Wings Volume I, III,* and *V*, as well as *Flesh Like Smoke, The Lemon Herberts, Wicked Tales,* and in magazines like *Weird Fiction Review, Dark Corridor, Nameless* and others. A life-long Lovecraftian, he has written critical articles that have appeared in *Lovecraft Studies, Crypt of Cthulhu, Weird Fiction Review, Nameless* and more. An expert on the life and work of pioneering science fiction writer William Hope Hodgson, Gafford is currently working on a book-length critical biography of Hodgson. Recently, he wrote *Some Notes on a Non-Entity: The Life of H.P. Lovecraft*, which is a 120-page graphic novel biography of HPL and is currently being illustrated by Jason Eckhardt for PS Publishing. The HPL graphic novel is scheduled for release in 2017. Gafford has a collection of short horror fiction, *The Dreamer in Fire and Other Tales*, coming from Hippocampus Press in 2017. A pop culture junkie, Gafford has probably watched far more TV than anyone should. He lives in Rhode Island with his long-suffering wife and three ambivalent cats.

Glenn, Teel James

Teel James Glenn has traveled the world for forty years as a stuntman, fight choreographer, swordmaster, jouster, illustrator, storyteller, bodyguard, actor and haunted house barker. One of the things he's proudest of is having studied sword under Errol Flynn's last stunt double. Teel's stories have been printed in numerous magazines, including *Weird Tales, Spinetingler, MAD, Black Belt, Fantasy Tales, Pulp Empire, Sherlock Holmes Mystery, Sixgun Western, Fantasy World Geographic, Silver Blade Quarterly, Tales of Old, Another Realm, AfterburnSF, Blazing Adventures,* and scores of others. His work has also appeared in three dozen books and anthologies, including *Monster Aces II*, edited by Jim Beard. He is also the winner of the 2012 Pulp Ark Award for Best Author. His website is: theurbanswashbuckler.com

Hall, Shannon

Cover artist Shannon Hall is an illustrator who specializes in various mediums. He has long wanted to be a comic book artist, but was repeatedly told that he would never make it with a wife and four kids. But his consistent response has been, quote: "Eat my shorts." (Update: He still hasn't made it.)

Hansen, Nancy

An avid reader and prolific writer of fantasy and adventure fiction for more than 25 years, Nancy A. Hansen is the author of the novels *Fortune's Pawn, Prophecy's Gambit, Master's Endgame,* and *Forged By Flame;* novellas *Companion Dragon's Tales: A Familiar Name* and *Copper's Choice;* and co-author of *Finding Waxy.* She has contributed to several anthologies, including *Tales of the Vagabond Bards, The Huntress of Greenwood* and *The Windriders of Everice.* Her short stories have been featured in multiple issues of Pro Se Presents, and several Pro Se anthologies as well: *The New Adventures of Senorita Scorpion, Tall Pulp, The New Adventures of the Whirlwind, Monster Aces Volume Two,* and *Singularity: Rise of the Posthumans.* Her e-story, *To Rule the Sky,* is one of Pro Se's Single Shot series. Nancy has contributed stories to Airship 27's *Sinbad: The New Voyages Volume One* and Mechanoid Press' debut book, *Monster Earth,* as well as the charity anthologies *Legends of New Pulp, When the Shadow Sees the Sun,* and *The Lost Children.* She is also the author of the debut novel in her Airship 27 pirate series, *Jezebel Johnson, Devil's Handmaid*. Nancy currently resides on an old farm in the beautiful rural environs of eastern Connecticut with an eclectic cast of family members and one very spoiled dog.

Spurlock, Duane

Duane Spurlock was raised by a long line of long-winded storytellers. He illustrated Brian Showers' *Bleeding Horse and Other Ghost Stories*, which won the Dracula Society's Children of the Night award. El Puno de Bronce (The Fist of Bronze), the luchador protagonist of "Whispers from the Dread World," previously appeared in a story entitled "Three Witches."

Reese, Barry

Barry Reese has spent the last fifteen years writing for publishers like Marvel Comics, West End Games, Moonstone Books and Pro Se Productions. He's best known for creating a shared universe of pulp adventure novels, most notably, the tales of Lazarus Gray, The Peregrine and Gravedigger. He can be found online at barryreese.net

ALSO AVAILABLE FROM

FLINCH! BOOKS

THE MIDNIGHT GUARDIAN: HOUR OF DARKNESS

Aided by technology decades ahead of its time, a masked hero emerges on the streets of Union City in the 1930s to stop a sociopathic crime lord's rampage of terror.

"Get this book. New Pulp doesn't get any better than this."
–William Patrick Maynard, Black Gate

BIG TOP TALES: SIX NEW TALES OF CIRCUS ADVENTURE

Follow the Henderson & Ross Royal Circus on a coast-to-coast journey of mystery, mayhem and murder during its 1956 summer season.

"…a stellar collection…Highly recommended."
–Ron Fortier, Pulp Fiction Reviews

SOMETHING STRANGE IS GOING ON: NEW TALES FROM THE FLETCHER HANKS UNIVERSE

Ten new stories spotlighting characters originally conceived by one of the most offbeat creators from the Golden Age of comics.

"…a tribute to the man's twisted, warped genius."
–The British Fantasy Society

FLINCH! BOOKS

Available on
AMAZON.COM
and
BARNESANDNOBLE.COM

www.ingramcontent.com/pod-product-compliance
Lightning Source LLC
Chambersburg PA
CBHW060937180626
46817CB00004B/1588